12/90
of the
Stop and the
of the '60's!
Much love,
Jack and Gayle

THE FURTHER INQUIRY

KEN KESEY

PHOTOGRAPHS BY RON BEVIRT

VIKING

VIKING

Published by the Penguin Group

Viking Penguin, a division of Penguin Books USA Inc.,

375 Hudson Street, New York, New York 10014, U.S.A.

Penguin Books Ltd, 27 Wrights Lane, London W8 5TZ, England

Penguin Books Australia Ltd, Ringwood, Victoria, Australia

Penguin Books Canada Ltd, 2801 John Street, Markham, Ontario, Canada L3R 1B4

Penguin Books (N.Z.) Ltd, 182–190 Wairau Road, Auckland 10, New Zealand

Penguin Books Ltd, Registered Offices: Harmondsworth, Middlesex, England

First published in 1990 by Viking Penguin, a division of Penguin Books USA Inc.

10 9 8 7 6 5 4 3 2 1

Copyright © Ken Kesey, 1990

Copyright © Ronald Bevirt, 1990

All rights reserved

Photographs on pages 86–87 and 165 by permission of Allen Ginsberg. © Allen Ginsberg.

Photographs comprising "flipbook" courtesy of the author.

Library of Congress Cataloging in Publication Data

Kesey, Ken.

The further inquiry / Ken Kesey.

p.   cm.

ISBN 0-670-83174-3

I. Title.

PS3561.E667F8   1990

813'.54—dc20   89-40685

Printed in Japan

Set in Bodoni and Futura Heavy

Designed by Michael Ian Kaye

—to Neal, and Page, and
Gordon, and Bubbles,
and Cass, and Tramp,
and Janice, and Pigpen,
and Tim, and Billy,
and other casualties
from this vector . . .

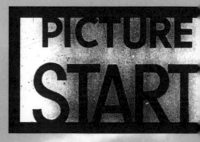

PICTURE
START

Also by Ken Kesey:

One Flew Over the Cuckoo's Nest
Sometimes a Great Notion
Kesey's Garage Sale
Demon Box
Tricker the Squirrel Meets Big Double the Bear
Caverns (with O. U. Levon)

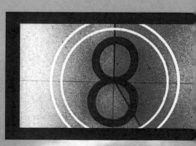

Interior. Dark. Big green leaves . . . looking through the leaves at a semi-obscured man in the background. He is wearing the old-fashioned legal robe and wig of a Victorian courtroom bailiff.

BAILIFF

We have a verdict then?

Through these leaves the V-meter comes into view, its polished walnut cabinet and brass-set dials gleaming in the courtroom gloom. The largest dial is divided simply into two areas: FOR— AGAINST. *The dial hand is quavering in the "*AGAINST.*"*

BAILIFF

Nothing further from the opposer?

Opposer Chest is walking away from the bailiff to a sign above an urn. NO SMOKING DURING INQUIRY. *He strikes a match across the sign.*

CHEST

Nothing, I guess, except—

He turns around, lighting a long cigar. The court opposer is a stout-faced, healthy man with thick round glasses and an un-blinking impishness to his gaze. With his wig cocked and his robe held girded at the middle to save the hem, he looks more a jovial monk than a judge advocate. He finishes lighting his cigar and blows a cloud of smoke across the courtroom.

—condolences.

BAILIFF

From the Defender?

Defender Tooey is a woman. She is less middle-aged than Chest, and prettier. Blond locks hang from beneath the tight white curls of her wig. She scoots back from her table and stands, as tall and lean as her adversary is otherwise. She waves tiredly at the cigar smoke.

TOOEY

Nay, nothing further.

BAILIFF

Adjourned then? So it is recorded . . .

The bailiff bangs his gavel. The hands on the V-meter dials are jarred violently.

Prepare the court for the next inquiry . . .

A rubber glove reaches into the leaves to tear away leads that have been attached to the plant. The hands on the meters pin into the red of all categories, then abruptly swing back to neutral and remain motionless.

The bailiff removes his wig, sits behind his little podium and begins unwrapping a bagel-and-sprout sandwich. The technician picks up the plant, his rubber-gloved hands roughly reaching through the leaves to grasp the plant's ornate copper pot. He carries it into the dim COURT OFFICIALS ONLY *area. Another attendant secures the V-meter.*

Beyond the witness stand is a large wooden table on casters. The table is piled with dusty Dictaphone rolls, plus an antique Dictaphone with a speaker horn. This apparatus is unplugged from the vicinity of the V-meter and the whole table is rolled away.

A female guard passes, striding toward the defendant's docket. She is husky and sexy in a khaki kibbutz uniform. Her long bare legs are tan and muscled. Her combat boots thump on the floor as she crosses the courtroom.

The courtroom is vast and dim, starkly furnished with the necessary accoutrements. Rows of old wooden church pews serve as seats; a threadbare carpet in the aisle leads to the heavy double door at the court's rear; the windowless blockstone walls are wainscoted with the same dark walnut used in the door and the pillars and the V-meter cabinetting; on the massive wall pillars simple wall fixtures cast somber pyramids of light. The ceiling's height is indeterminate due to the dim lighting, but it is apparently quite lofty. An old four-blade ceiling fan hangs by its pole in the dimness, rotating lugubriously, its ancient motor whirring. The witnesses that have been seated in the pews below are rising and moving toward the middle aisle to leave. They are old, attired in solemn black suits or dresses. Many of the women are veiled. Some of the men are donning fedoras and heavy fur-collared overcoats as they rise to depart. They do not speak or look at each other as they meet in the aisle, but move solemnly on toward the double door. One old man turns to look back. He is hatless and his black suit is very worn. A carnation dribbles petals down his lapel as he thumbs his tooth toward a hooded figure being escorted by the guard through a dark door marked DOWN. The door closes behind this dim defendant with an echoing bong. The old man turns and follows the others toward the courtroom door.

Opposer Chest pulls out the bottom drawer of a filing cabinet. The drawer is labeled B—BEHAN to BZYNCXI. He refiles the case just heard, the very last in the drawer. Behind these files is a nearly empty pint.

CHEST

Last of the B's and the booze, Defender Tooey.

Miss Tooey, at her own cabinet, filing away her own record, answers without turning from her task:

TOOEY

Perhaps a drop in my coffee, thank you Opposer Chest
. . . to calm my gastrics.

They slam their respective drawers. As they both stand stiffly the files are wheeled away and two new ones wheeled in. Tooey pulls out the top drawer of the new cabinet. Chest sticks his

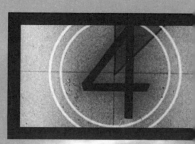

*cigar in his mouth, picks her half full coffee mug from her table
and tosses its contents into the sand urn. He pours in nearly
half the whiskey, checks the bottle, adds a bit more to be fair
. . . all the while talking around the cigar clinched in his teeth:*

CHEST

Five "Againsts" in a row, eh?

*He sets her cup on her table and reaches for his water glass.
It has a cigar butt stuck down into the ice cubes. Without hes-
itating he sets the glass aside and pours the remainder of the
bottle directly into his half full water pitcher. He tosses the
bottle into the urn and hefts the pitcher by its handle.*

Well cheer up; isn't your hitch nearly finished?

*Tooey picks up the cup and pulls out the next drawer in her
bank of files.*

TOOEY

This'll be my last for the session, halleluia. Defending
unsettles me, win or lose.

*She takes out the first dossier and sits. The drawer is marked
C—CASSADY to COLSON. Chest lifts his pitcher to her in toast.*

CHEST

Then it's for a calm and quick one, I pray, Miss Tooey.

*Without looking up from the cover of the dossier, Tooey lifts
her coffee cup in Chest's direction.*

TOOEY

I also, Mr. Chest.

*Still standing at his cabinet, Chest removes his cigar and drinks,
looking out over the rim of the pitcher, surveying the new as-
sortment of witnesses filing down the aisle and taking seats.
They aren't as old as the departing gangsters, or as sinister—
they are dressed much more casually—but they are just as sol-*

emn and subdued. And while they all seem to be acquainted they don't sit next to each other. They speak only to mutter apologies as they have to pass each other, seeking the murkiest seats in the pews. Through the glass rim of his up-tilting pitcher Chest perceives the faces as warped and twisted. He lowers the pitcher, beginning to frown at what he sees:

CHEST
Though I somehow have my doubts that it will so be, Miss Tooey . . .

Tooey's hand has been tracing down the cover of the dossier. From the name of Cassady, Neal, through ALIAS *Moriarity, Dean;* ALIAS *Pomeroy, Cody;* ALIAS *Kennedy, Hart;* ALIAS *Houlihan, Dean . . . tracing on down to the last* ALIAS—*Speed Limit, Sir—below which is a snapshot: a man in a bright polo shirt strains and grimaces lewdly, carrying a huge wooden cross up a hill.*

TOOEY
I also, Mr. Chest, I also.

NEAL CASSADY
IN THE
BACKHOUSE

The clashing of lockworks across the courtroom lifts Tooey's head. A door marked WAITING *is being assailed by an attendant with a clipboard and a big ring of keys. There are three locks on the door and the attendant is trying to find the right keys. The guard beside the door maintains a buxom attention. The attendant is very clumsy and slow with his keys. The courtroom watches, mesmerized. Chest removes his cigar, and blows smoke toward the door. The attendant gets it unlocked. The guard steps forward, twists the knob, and pulls it open to reveal a long corridor. Hooded figures line the wall on both sides, their dim faces leaning forward to look towards the door.*

ATTENDANT

Cassady, Neal, alias Moriarity, Dean, alias Pomeroy, Cody, alias—

The reading is interrupted by a hooded figure standing up into the doorway, suddenly—

CASSADY'S SPIRIT

All present and accounted for sirrah, officer . . . *(saluting burlesquely, robe much too large to see hands)* yer honor, highness, who-ness, hoop!

The spirit ogles the guard lewdly, roused to a jerking frenzy by her ample appearance in the tight shorts.

Tooey takes a fortifying sip from her cup and looks at the next page of her dossier, sighing. Chest gapes at the apparition:

CHEST

Who's benching this beauty for us, anyway? Not another Aunt Fancy's favorite fuchsia, I'll bet . . .

TOOEY *(correcting him)*

Ficus philodendron.

The spirit is being pushed toward the docket by the guard. He is trying to break her icy attitude by pointing out various witnesses seated in the courtroom.

SPIRIT

There's Chloe, facing the African night . . . there's lovely Sensuous X on the right. There's Peter Orlovsky, there with all the hair. Ginsberg, clean that boy up! Where are we? Oh, there's Dale Kesey. Dale. Yes, and here's Mike, y'know, that you girls better watch out for.

Bang! The gavel swings all heads to bailiff standing, adjusting his wig, balling up his lunch litter—:

BAILIFF

All rise All rise All rise.

He bangs his gavel three more times and looks over his shoulder into the dark beyond the bench.

Everyone stands, looking past the judge's bench. Tooey has the paper out of the envelope and is smiling slightly at what she reads.

TOOEY

No, Mr. Chest. Neither flora nor fauna. Seated in judgment for this beauty we have a machine.

A rolldoor is rolled up, very violently and loudly. Attendants and trustees in the same official-but-rumpled lab-tech frocks walk in from the darkness. They are hauling on two huge ropes. The grill of the bus looms into view. Enormous, garish, and incredibly dilapidated. A sad pop, and a hissing; the right front has blown, slanting the bus ludicrously as the tire hisses empty. The sign at the top slants, bringing into view the name FURTHER.

The bailiff permits everyone to be seated with a rap of gavel.

The courtroom audience sink to their seats, staring at the decaying vehicle.

The V-meter technician wheels his apparatus to the front of the bus as his rubber-gloved assistant opens the hood.

Rubber Glove reaches leads to battery poles, grinding them through spider webs and corrosion to get some contact . . .

RUBBER GLOVE

Anything?

WHITE GLOVE

Nada . . .

He gives the face of his machine a quick backhand.

The Amazonian guard opens the latch of the gate to the docket and ushers the hooded spirit to the defendant's seat. Muttering, the spirit watches the technicians trying to get a reading from the bus.

WHITE GLOVE

Still nada, amigo . . .

SPIRIT *(whispering)*

Try the tire . . .

As though he'd heard, Rubber Glove steps back from the decayed innards of the bus motor in frustrated disgust and kicks the tire.

The dials quaver.

WHITE GLOVE

A touch, I'll admit, a touch . . .

Chest and Tooey are at their tables, going over their dossiers. They read very fast; they reach the bottom of each page and turn to the next almost simultaneously.

Into the area where the big Dictaphone table had been is wheeled a huge KEM* apparatus with three blank viewing screens. Except for the glass screens and chrome capstans the machine is made of the same heavy walnut. A long cord is reeled from beneath it and coupled with a big 3-phase socket at the base of the V-meter. The three screens come on. White Glove removes

a can of film from a file cabinet and blows dust from it. Rubber Glove slams the bus hood. The dials of the meter all jump.

Chest and Tooey are still turning pages together. Chest stops. He raises his head and begins to smile. He's figured his case. His colleague continues to read on.

The bailiff watches Tooey, his gavel raised . . .

> **BAILIFF**
> With permission of the Defender . . . ?

Tooey holds up her hand. She is now beginning to smile. Finally she closes the dossier.

> **TOOEY**
> The Defense is ready, Bailiff . . .

The gavel bangs.

The dials quaver.

> **BAILIFF**
> The inquiry is open have a care and govern yourselves accordingly. Opposition, will you present your case?

Chest stands, looking up out of his dossier.

> **CHEST**
> Sebern? A Mister Sebern in the court?

> **BAILIFF**
> Mr. Sebern . . . ?

> **ROY**
> Here. Roy Sebern here.

Roy stands and walks up aisle. Beyond him in the background, the screens of the KEM fill, one after the other, with pictures of Roy from bus days, 25 years earlier. Roy stops before the bailiff's podium and turns. His "now" face is flanked by 3 out-of-focus bearded "then" faces. He is a hawkishly-featured man with black hair and eyebrows. His eyes are intense behind black-rimmed glasses.

BAILIFF

How would you be called by this court?

ROY

Roy will be fine.

Gavel points to the witness seat and Roy sits. Chest comes forward, putting his cigar in its ashtray.

CHEST

Mr. Roy ah . . . what would you say is your occupation at present?

ROY

I would have to say it is . . . artist.

CHEST

A title not taken lightly by you, I can see.

ROY

I am serious about it if that's what you mean.

CHEST

Precisely what I mean. Now Roy, we would like to inquire about a certain journey by bus that took place across the United States of America in the summer of *(rifling through his papers)* 1964?

The three screens on the KEM are beginning to spin, forward and back, searching randomly among Roy footage.

ROY

Sixty-four, yes. Way back there.

CHEST

The bus, way back there, must have looked somewhat different than *this. (Chest jerks his chin toward the decrepit bus parked behind them.)*

ROY

Its earliest, its first look was plain school bus yellow—

A reel rolls on KEM table, producing a shot of yellow bus on a green, dewy morn. There is an outdoor sound of kids laughing, birds singing, men hammering and calling to each other in general activity, overlaid throughout with strains of Coltrane's "Greensleeves."

ROY *(voice-over)*

When I first heard Kesey say we were going to paint it the idea didn't appeal to me at all. Because I thought it looked really fine the way it was . . . I didn't see any reason to obliterate it.

CHEST *(voice-over)*

Did you try to discourage this obliteration?

ROY *(voice-over) beginning to speak faster, getting irritated without being certain why:* I may have just mentioned in passing . . . but once it was obvious it was going to happen, I just jumped in with everybody else. I'd been paying attention to abstract expressionism, in other words, "having at" whatever you were painting and just kind of flinging the paint at the canvas.

ROY *(voice-over)*

And this bus was a canvas that you could keep "having at" all the way to New York. The longest painting in painting history—

CHEST *(voice-over)*

New York?

ROY *(voice-over)*

Where the bus was headed. To the World's Fair . . .

* Kem-Keller Electronic Machine

CHEST

That was its goal?

ROY

Partially. Something more than that though, something—

CHEST

Further?

Roy doesn't answer. He is watching himself on the KEM paint on the FURTHER sign.

ROY *(voice-over)*

I had this very strong feeling that having a name like Further would contribute impetus to keeping it going,—when it might get stuck, or broken down— that the word would have *power*—like Shazam. . . .

CHEST *(voice-over)*

And did your "magic word" in fact *serve* as such on the trip, Roy?

ROY

I can't really say. I wasn't on the bus.

CHEST

Not *on* the bus!? After you had been with it from its virgin yellow to its burgeoning beauty? After you had named it—?

ROY

I had been to New York recently. I didn't feel like making another trip.

CHEST

Even on the longest painting in history?

Roy doesn't answer. He turns instead to look at the hooded figure in the defendant's dock.

CHEST *(voice-over)*

You were apprehensive? About the driver?

ROY

I didn't know that Cassady was driving until I saw him come tearing up, that afternoon . . .

16 mm from top of bus, looking toward road going past La Honda bridge.

KESEY *(voice-over)*

Hagen! Here he comes. Get his entrance!

A beat-up Studebaker comes steaming around the corner, past the bridge. It screeches to a dusty stop and reverses for another try. Hagen is struggling to set up his tripod and camera. He gets it secured and running just as the Studebaker shifts out of reverse and comes rumbling across the bridge right at it. The car passes too close and the point of view of Hagen's camera goes flying, then lies still, shooting serenely up into the leaves . . . as the sound of Cassady's arrival continues rattling on, and "Love Potion No. 9" plays in the background from his car radio.

KESEY *(voice-over)*

Well I hope we got that entrance. Hagen was right in the—Hagen? Hagen!

Back in courtroom, Chest is closing in on Roy.

CHEST

So you had a "strong feeling" about riding to New York in a bus driven by a man of Mr. Cassady's reputation?

ROY

Wild driving wasn't the only thing that Cassady had a reputation for. He had already been in San Quentin a couple of years.

CHEST

For?

ROY
Drugs. Drugs and driving. I didn't want to do time for anybody's indulgences. So I didn't get on the bus.

His voice trails off. He stares at shots of the bus being painted, the colors hypnotically surging and blending. Chest starts to reach for his smoking cigar, then remembers the inquiry is still in progress.

CHEST
Your witness, Miss Tooey . . .

TOOEY
Nothing for now, thank you, Roy.

BAILIFF *(bangs gavel)*
The witness will step down. Next.

CHEST
Chloe Keighly-Peach Scott.

Chloe rises from a pew and walks to the stand, passing Roy on his way down.

BAILIFF
And how would you be called?

CHLOE
Chloe will be just fine, thank you.

CHEST
And your occupation?

CHLOE
Dancer, teacher, movement therapist . . . dancer.

CHEST
Then and now?

CHLOE
And forever, I fancy.

Chest is looking at shots on KEM of Chloe dancing.

CHEST *(smiling, charmed)*
Chloe, with your permission, you seem uncommonly—ah

CHLOE *(voice-over)*
Uncommon? I suppose it is my English upbringing.

CHEST *(voice-over)*
How then—could you tell us—did you become involved with these—

CHLOE *(voice-over)*
Commoners? Well, I met them at Stanford in 1958.

CHEST *(voice-over)*
You were associated with the university?

CHLOE *(voice-over)*
Working in the dean's office. Secretary of fraternities. Ken and most of the others were students or grad students. Stanfordites. Very educated.

A party on the KEM; black and white; rhythm and blues; Cassady, shirtless and shameless, racketing and rapping.

CHEST *(voice-over)*

And Mr. Cassady?

CHLOE *(voice-over)*

An eighth-grade education . . . in a rat grade school,

he used to claim. But not illiterate, not a bit of it. He could quote pages of Proust verbatim.

CHEST *(voice-over)*

I'm sure he could. But I meant when did you first make his acquaintance?

CHLOE *(voice-over)*

I can't actually remember the first time I saw him.
Probably a party and Neal just came . . .

CHEST *(voice-over)*

Some time before the excursion in question?

CHLOE *(voice-over)*

Oh yes. Months. Maybe years. In the wine and bongo
time.

CHEST *(voice-over)*

Can you tell us something of your impressions of Mr.
Cassady by the time this colorful expedition was
mounted?

CHLOE *(voice-over)*

Well, by the time of this colorful expedition, and well
before that too, I hadn't really gotten along very well
with Mr. Cassady.

CHEST *(voice-over)*

Why was that?

On one of the partying KEM screens, Cassady is standing, jerk-ing dementedly, atop a barstool.

CHLOE *(voice-over)*

He sort of frightened me. He seemed to be coming from
someplace so different from where I think I—and most
people—come from. It made it difficult to communi-
cate with him, to talk. A difficulty amplified terrifically
by the additional fact that *he* never shut up.

CHEST *(voice-over)*

Never?

CHLOE *(voice-over)*

Never. But I will say this: sometimes the things he was
talking, well it was amazing.

Two images of Cassady have begun to jabber all at once. Chloe's voice has to rise to speak over the cacophony.

> It was as if he were actually talking to everybody in the room at the same time, referring to something they were doing, or thinking, or had been doing or thinking an instant before, or in a past life, or in a life to come. And then, with all the dope stuff going on, and him taking everything, and about ten times as much of it as anybody else . . .

Two images stop jabbering as the third topples from a barstool.

CHLOE

He was just too *reckless* to be my cup of tea . . . even on solid ground, and *especially* behind the wheel of a vehicle I was traveling in.

CHEST

But you did get on the bus?

The party pictures are replaced by shots of Leaving Day and leaving day Coltrane sound.

CHLOE *(voice-over)*

I wanted to go east that summer. And I didn't have much money, and it was a free ride. But I knew I was going to jump ship after about twenty-four hours. Why we ran out of gas before we'd even crossed the bridge out of La Honda! And everybody milling about in a chemical frenzy. You couldn't sleep, you couldn't even relax and watch the scenery it was such a mad melee. In fact, the only time it would quiet down was when a cop would pull us over . . .

A red light rotates in the desert morning. The bus and a California Highway Patrol car parley while oil is sucked from the flat landscape by great bobbing oilsuckers. The patrol car pulls

away. The bus full of relieved passengers join in a Dragnet "dum da dum dum."

CHEST
So you jumped ship in—

CHLOE
San Luis Obispo. Before we even reached L.A.

CHEST
What were your thoughts about getting off the bus at this early stage in the expedition?

CHLOE
My thoughts were, "Thank God I'm not crossing the country in that rolling madhouse!"

The bus pulls out after the cop leaves.

CHLOE *(voice-over)*
I swear, I've been on better Mexican busses. With pigs and chickens and drunk drivers who acted more civilized!

CHEST *(voice-over)*
But it was mostly the driver.

Bus interior. Chaos. Fervor. Then, a stop at a burger stand.

CHLOE *(voice-over)*
And the noise. And the overcrowding. And no rest stops except breakdowns. And eating nothing but rat-burgers. . . . There was always plenty of money but I think they must have actually liked ratburgers. It fit in with the rest of the motifs and decor of the trip.

CHEST
Which was?

CHLOE
Rat grade. Basic rat grade.

Cassady's spirit jerks at this, stung. But he leans close to the guard and confides:

SPIRIT
Chloe. Being herself. She's a redhead, see?

CHEST
Thank you, Chloe. Miss Tooey?

TOOEY *(without standing)*
Let me get this clear, dear; you chose to jump ship and . . . cross the country by some more civilized means?

CHLOE
TWA. To New York where I was able to stay at this nice big flat on 73rd.

TOOEY
Did you see the bus again?

CHLOE

Where do you think it headed for as soon as it arrived? Like a pig for the pantry . . .

TOOEY

But you did get back on?

CHLOE

Right. It only took me a half a day to jump ship that time.

TOOEY

Thank you Chloe. Nothing else from me.

Chloe starts to rise as the bailiff lifts his gavel. Chest interrupts.

CHEST

A moment . . . *(looking at a note in his ever-growing wad of papers)* . . . does the name Stark Naked mean anything to you?

CHLOE

Isn't that what they came to call the poor child—I can't recall her name—that went—Oh, is she here?

CHEST

No, she isn't. But never mind. You've been very helpful.

BAILIFF

You may step down, Mrs. Keighly-Peach Scott.

CHLOE *(stepping down)*

Chloe will be quite adequate.

CHEST

John Babbs?

While John is coming forward to take the stand, Chest notices Tooey is irritated by the smoke of his cigar.

I'm sorry. Let me put that out!

Chest picks up the tray and cigar, but before he puts it out he is distracted by a mischievous thought and sits on Tooey's desk to ask her:

Say, just who *was* this guy Cassady? How did he die? What were his last words?

Tooey returns his grin, and speaks over her shoulder to one of her aides:

TOOEY

Jenny, check the Rosebud Records, wouldn't you . . . ?

Chest moves away, examining his notes. The ashtray is left where it was, still smoking.

CHEST

To continue further with witnesses that seem to have been both not on the bus *and* not off the bus—John,

it seems you are also among those who jumped ship before this cruise was ended.

JOHN

I think I can proudly state that I rode it out to the end.

CHEST

But my records indicate—

JOHN

Maybe not all the way there and back—

CHEST

—also, that you were even nicknamed "Sometimes Missing."

JOHN *(voice-over)*

—but at least all the way there. The name was acquired because I got off the bus and went into a drugstore and when I came back it was gone. I hitchhiked after it for days.

On screen John is just being picked up.

CHEST *(voice-over)*

They were so disorganized?

JOHN *(voice-over)*

I felt almost that it was a *deliberate* disorganization—prank, if you will—to stir up some excitement. . . . But you see this is in Virginia. Much farther east than where Chloe jumped ship, but not as far as where I finally *got* off . . .

Chest, turning away in exasperation, calls to one of the attendants in the background.

CHEST

Give us a map.

An attendant rolls up a rack full of map rollers. He pulls down first a map of the solar system, then a map of an alien continent, then a map of the United States. The attendant gives Chest a pointer. Chest hands it on to John.

If you please . . .

> **JOHN** *(voice-over)*
> Virginia is *here*. We were headed *here* and Chloe got off about *here*, just about L.A. . . .

With each point a screen of the KEM (in background, beneath hanging map) lights up. First the middle, with a hold frame of John in Virginia, then the left, with a hold of the N.Y. skyline, then the right with shots of L.A. These L.A. shots are moving. There are street sounds.

> *(looking at middle KEM frame of himself, musing:)*
> Maybe not deliberate, but it could have been a symbolic gesture . . .

Inside the bus: a woman's rear looms as she bends over in white shorts. It is spray-painted Day-Glo blue, a circle and an eye on each buttock.

> **CHEST** *(voice-over)*
> They were capable of leaving behind one of their own number? Heartlessly abandoning him to whatever fate chance might afford?

The L.A. street sounds get louder. The L.A. freeway is seen out the bus window.

> **JOHN** *(raising his voice over bus furor:)* This is L.A. That's Hagen getting film for the great movie we were all making. Finally heading east . . .

The 16mm point of view is whipping the freeway sights to a frenzied froth.

In the courtroom audience Hagen watches, sunk down in his pew. Garcia leans over from the pew behind and whispers:

GARCIA

What did you shoot this with, Hagen? A tommy gun?

HAGEN

Yeh. And it looks like I just wounded it.

On the stand John is watching the KEM and listening to himself make a speech over the roar of the bus. "We're gonna win! Just remember the word Sacrifice! Sacrifice! Glorious, and in Vain . . ."

JOHN

And I didn't mean heartless. Overall I think there was a lot of loyalty and nobody would have been deserted. I just know I finally had to get away. My desire to spend every possible moment on a bus full of drug-crazed moviemakers driven by the ex-king of the beat-niks lessened somewhat in the distance between L.A. and New York.

CHEST *(voice-over)*

This lady here, John, did she make it to New York?

On the KEM, a shot of Stark holds. Cassady's spirit draws a breath:

SPIRIT

Excuse me for living, O dear God, for presuming. There she is: Stark Naked herself. Yes, my one orgasm on the trip. Or two. She left us early.

The female guard leans slightly out from her parade rest stance to get a better look at the KEM, interested in spite of herself.

JOHN

Stark was brought on board by Michael Hagen. Maybe you ought to talk to him about her disembarkation.

In the pews Hagen is suddenly alert. It's obvious that it's him they're talking about and that the direction of the questioning should call him next. He half rises, hoping to sneak out down the pews past Page who's sitting half-asleep. Page is wearing one of the black robes like the Cassady spirit.

CHEST
Next I'd like to call—(*looking up from his pages*)—
Mr. Page Browning, please.

Hagen stops, relieved; Page is suddenly wide-eyed and worried. Hagen resumes his seat. Page rises apprehensively.

(*aside to Tooey:*) Apparently there were not only some not on and not off but not even *let* on as well.

Page is being sworn in. He keeps looking at the KEM, fearfully, waiting for images of himself to appear as they have in corre-

*spondence with the previous witnesses. Chest appears at Page's
side:*

> With your permission.

Page snaps to attention, looking straight ahead.

PAGE

Yes sir.

CHEST

Could you tell us your name please?

PAGE

Yes sir. John Page Browning.

CHEST

As you're undoubtedly aware, we're investigating a
piece from the record of Mr. Neal Cassady, and I'd
like to ask you how you first made his acquaintance.

PAGE

I don't remember.

CHEST

Was not Mr. Cassady an unforgettable figure in your
life?

PAGE

No sir. Yes sir.

CHEST

That's very interesting. Tell me, Mr. Browning, what
did you know of Mr. Cassady's prior record with re-
gard to the law?

PAGE

Nothing.

CHEST

I see. Ah, at the time when you first made his acquaintance, what was your own record like with re-
gard to the law?

PAGE

I had none.

CHEST

You had no record, no arrests of any kind?

PAGE

Yes sir. No sir.

CHEST

Well, Mr. Browning, though this is not your inquiry—
yet—we have evidence to the contrary here. Perhaps
you'd like to dispute it but the record shows that you
were arrested for smuggling all through the early six-
ties, and in 1965 *convicted* for possession of certain
substances that were illegal at the time. Do you rec-
ollect this?

PAGE

Sixty-five? Let me see . . .

CHEST

Maybe you are aware also that Mr. Cassady had a
similar arrest on his record?

PAGE

No sir, no.

CHEST

You *were* aware that Mr. Cassady employed drugs that
were illegal.

PAGE

He did what?

CHEST

He used drugs that were illegal.

PAGE

He did?

The white-gloved technician watches his V-meter dials, smiling as Page's lies register.

> **CHEST**
> Your naivete is dazzling, Mr. John Page Browning.

During this time the KEM has been running footage to the contrary, of substances being smoked and potions being drunk. Especially shots of a lemonade jug. As this juice jug is tipped up, a radio can be heard in the background playing "Love Potion No. 9." Page is torn between paying attention to Chest on the one side and the flickering, contradictory KEM on the other.

> **PAGE**
> Yes sir.

> **CHEST** *(looking at the KEM)*
> By the by, John Page, I've noticed evidence of your presence before and after this excursion, but not during.

> **PAGE**
> I didn't go to New York, no sir. I did get on later. When we went to Mexico.

> **CHEST**
> You jumped ship also? For fear of your safety under the steerage of Mr. Cassady?

> **PAGE**
> No sir! I always felt good about riding with Neal. I know his driving style drove a lot of people crazy but I liked it.

> **CHEST**
> Then why did you miss the trip?

PAGE

They didn't want me on! They were afraid if a cop pulled over the bus that me, with my record, would draw heat and they—

CHEST *(smiling at Page's slip)*

Didn't let you on the bus?

PAGE

I don't remember.

CHEST

Don't remember . . . *(he squints at his record notes)* then you probably don't even recall the events that occasioned your own demise . . . ?

PAGE

Oh, sure, I remember that. Too much vodka trying to come down off a speed run. The same mistake like your other— . . . like other guys probably made.

CHEST

Mr. Browning, you may step down. With my sincere commendation *and* sympathy.

PAGE

What for?

CHEST

For your loyalty, John Page. Defender Tooey?

TOOEY

Later perhaps . . .

CHEST

Then could I see now *(looking at his notes)* Miss Jane Burton, please?

Bus film begins to move on KEM as Jane rises from pews and comes to the witness stand. She towers over Chest as she strides past him.

BAILIFF

How would you be called?

JANE *(very hoarsely)*

Jane Burton.

CHEST

Is that Miss, or Mrs.?

JANE

Ms.

CHEST

Ms. Burton, you seem to have a very small voice for someone of your stature.

JANE

Heavy drinker and smoker.

CHEST

Could the court have the benefit of some amplification, please?

An attendant switches on a goosenecked mike. He bends it uncomfortably close to Jane's mouth as Chest goes over his notes on Jane.

A professor of philosophy? On a pleasure cruise to New York?

JANE

One of those Stanfordites, yes. And I can tell you right now it was the exact opposite of a pleasure palace.

CHEST

Good. Do tell us a little about the lifestyle on this bus.

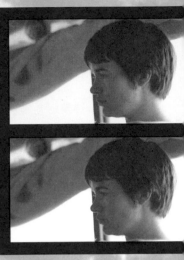
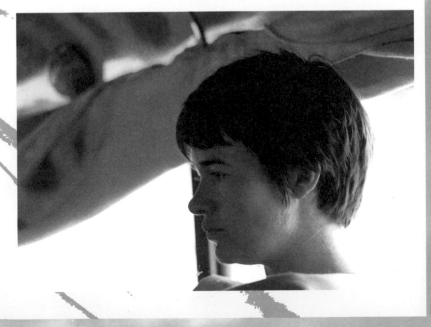

JANE

There was no lifestyle. Eating happened by accident. If you slept it was because you were lucky. You gotta realize I became especially cranky and uncomfortable because I was pregnant.

CHEST

Well, describe a little what the feelings were with these people.

JANE

Nobody was mad at each other. It's just that everything was always fouled up, all the time.

CHEST

What do you mean?

JANE

Well, the bus didn't run too good and we got lost all the time and all the equipment broke down. We had all the money in a plastic bag and I think a bunch of it got lost. We had all the acid in the lemonade jar and somebody guzzled half of it.

CHEST

Who was that?

JANE

That was what's her name . . . Kathy . . . Stark . . . who went crazy.

CHEST

Kathy . . . Stark . . . who went crazy?

JANE

Right.

CHEST

You're referring to lysergic acid diethylamide, I presume.

JANE

Oh yes, yes, Mr. Chest. Number 25.

CHEST

Now, Ms. Burton, if we could pick up where we were before Mr. Browning's testimony, I'd like to press further in your journey east.

Chest picks up the pointer and places its tip on the large map of the United States. The KEM rolls. A desert oasis simmers in the sun; a shallow stream trickles through the willows; frogs peep and birds sing and from the distance we hear an outraged "Oh no!"

JANE *(voice-over)*

Wikieup.

CHEST *(voice-over)*

Arizona, I believe.

A Day-Glo bus tire turns futilely in the sand. Cries of "Uh-oh" are heard over the straining engine. The camera pans across the disheveled Day-Glo roof to the back of the bus where Kesey joins George who is trying to push.

GEORGE

Definitely ominous.

JANE *(voice-over)*

Looks like we're digging in. Seems fairly typical.

KESEY

I haven't seen the back of it. How we looking here?

Cassady is out of the bus. He stands at the front of the mired vehicle and laughs at the impossibility of the situation.

JANE *(voice-over)*

Look at Neal, he's loving it. Every minute of it.

CHEST *(voice-over)*

He loves getting stuck in the sand?

JANE *(voice-over)*

He doesn't have any place to go. I had thought of this
as a way of getting to New York. Unlike other people.

*Pranksters wander around the bus. Zonk tosses a stone aim-
lessly. Kesey inspects the sunken tire. Cassady, carrying a long
stick, approaches Chuck who is on his hands and knees, digging.
Babbs stands aside.*

BABBS

It's all part of it.

CHUCK

That would be terrible if . . .

CASSADY
Oh, I stood and I fretted, I came up all sweated; I
said, I'll get out of this fucking hole, by god, or I'll . . .

*A beautiful brunette—Kathy-to-become-Stark—stands in the
doorway of the bus, holding her mandolin and purse. She is
loaded. The bus jostles back and forth. She perches herself in
the doorway and refuses to get off.*

HASSLER
If for no other reason than that I'm going to brain
you if you don't get out, get out!

*Stark starts to protest but is thrown off the bus. She drifts
toward the sand. The sound of the mandolin, forbidding and
weird, follows her.*

*Washed-out dissolves of her rolling in the sand while distant
voices echo in her head:*

CHEST *(voice-over)*

What is happening here? This man is holding out a lobster tail, Mr. Kesey is, I believe.

JANE *(voice-over)*

That's dinner.

CHEST *(voice-over)*

Dinner for twelve?

JANE *(voice-over)*

She's pretty out of it at this point.

CHEST *(voice-over)*

She's ingested a drug?

JANE *(voice-over)*

That *would* explain why she got only *one* lobster tail . . . the loaves-and-fishes syndrome.

STARK *(gesturing toward a swaggering Cassady:)* How can any man be so—

NEAL

What have you been doing all this time?

STARK

Goddammit!

NEAL

Playing yourself is hardly fair.

STARK *(wiping away tears)*

Oh, stupid.

NEAL

Well, I guess the old flute will have to do.

STARK

I broke that flute.

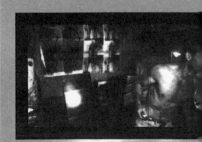

NEAL

You broke your flute? Well, why didn't you tell me it was important?

The mandolin twangs again. Neal moves closer to the stricken Stark.

Oh, it's a horrible thought I know, but we still can't play *that* flat.

At the back of the bus, Hassler turns from the bus tire.

HASSLER

Oh for the love of Jesus and His holy family and all their kids.

Stark plays her flute in the sand. The mandolin twangs. Gretchen laughs in the distance.

BABBS

It's Gretchen stretchin', she's mightly fetchin'. Always scratchin' kitchen matches, never itchin' chicken snatches.

HASSLER

I saw her once.

Babbs and Gretch play barefoot in the swamp. Day-Glo paint floats on a puddle.

HASSLER

We're painting the face of the nation.

A T-shirt is lifted from the puddle of paints. It is patterned a prehistoric tie dye.

BABBS

One thing I've learned is I'll never drink downstream from the Merry Pranksters' campsite.

Zonk is wearing the T-shirt. He dances, turning slowly. His back is covered with the paint. Jane is watching, sitting in the

shallow river in her dress. She stands, hikes up her dress and hygienically splashes her crotch.

> **JANE** *(speaking to her daughter in the courtroom audience:)* Look! There's my nice fat belly when I was carrying you, Emmy . . .

> **CHEST** *(looking with disapproval at the picture of Jane on the KEM:)* You were giving yourself a bath here? This is a public place, is it not?

> **JANE**
> Well, it wasn't really too public.

> **CHEST**
> I'm curious as to the reactions of the public, nevertheless.

> **JANE** *(voice-over)*
> My memory of that is that we were always received

fairly well by most people. A bunch of freaks going through the South, going through Texas especially, *could* have got in a lot of trouble.

Gretch is working her way from the nitty-gritty down to the grimy slimey.

Acid wasn't illegal or infamous, yet. Hippies or drug freaks never occurred to anybody. And then we *consciously* had a clean image.

Gretch's face flickers from repugnance to dismay, to horror; on through to the light on the other side; to relief, and to joy and finally, ecstasy.

JANE *(cont.)*

All short haircuts. Red, white and blue motif. We knew we would definitely pass that way. And I mean all of us were WASP college kids. Oh, this is good! Babbs and Gretch are just beginning one of the greatest acid highs known to history . . .

GRETCH

Eee-haw!

The tractor has arrived. The Pranksters rise from the mire and mud and race to meet it.

Babbs and then Gretch emerge with slime on their heads.

KESEY

That's Miss Slime of 1964.

The Pranksters chorus in reply: "Slime! Slime Queen!" The tractor is positioned behind the bus. Gretch becomes more ecstatic.

GRETCH

What more can a garbage can ask for than beautiful rubbish? You can scrubbish the rubbish.

Stark lies on the ground, hand on her breast, looking toward the bus, singing:

STARK

Compromise . . . while the rain comes down and kills a spider in the groin.

NEAL

Well, that's *not* a compromise, my dear . . .

   JANE *(courtroom voice-over)*

Poor Stark. This was miserable. Still the aspiring star-let trying to bear up under the glare of 2,000 micrograms.

Stark rises from her prone position and continues to sing to the camera.

STARK

With frogs hopping, hopping, and the bees that are kept in the beekeeper's hive must not go without stopping.

Neal's voice becomes clearer in the background, rapping in simultaneous syncopation with her singing:

NEAL

I've really found matches by god, by the score.

STARK

Oh yes, oh yes, oh sweet spon-*tai-a-ine*ous earth. How often have the fingers of prurient philosophers pinched and poked thee?

She pauses, full of nameless agonies.

STARK

Why doesn't Mike come help us now? We need your attention to bring us to the fore.

She appears to kiss the air and then looks away as her smile fades.

NEAL

That would have worked of course, *earlier*.

STARK

Earlier, yes, much earlier.

NEAL

Well, I think we could make you a real hit.

STARK

Ah yes, a hit. We're going to have a hit.

NEAL

Yessss. That's what we'll have to do.

STARK

We are going too h-i-i-i-gh.

NEAL

Now you just do everything I say and we'll give that producer a year and a half—

STARK

. . . like everything I do, of course it comes out . . .

The tractor waits to pull the bus. Sandy saunters past, sporting miles of microphone cables, wearing only his underwear. Babbs turns to the crew:

BABBS

Okay men! Cassady . . . behind the wheel, Neal!

The tractor man brings up the chains. Babbs hooks them beneath the bus.

KESEY

Look at that goddamn engine.

BABBS

Okay! Take it! Okay, move out of the way, Ron.

Babbs stands from the sand, the chain fastened from the back of the bus to the tractor. The tractor roars. Dale kneels in the sand and examines the progress. None.

BABBS

C'mon!

KESEY

C'mon, back 'er.

BABBS

Go! Go! Wait a minute. Wait a minute . . . he hasn't got it in reverse yet.

KESEY

You're *pulling against each other*!

Cassady laughs out the window of the bus and corrects the gear.

BABBS

Ready? . . . Okay, let's go with it! . . . C'mon!

KESEY
He's moving!

The tractor begins to make headway. Babbs leaps over the chain.

BABBS
We're going . . . Go!

The bus begins to move out of the hole. Babbs leaps and waves his arms. Kesey cheers. Stark comes running, drenched, from the river. The sleeves of her sweater are soaked with sand and water and hang off the ends of her arms like flowery tentacles. They flail the air as she pirouettes in random looney joy.

The tractor has pulled the bus out on high ground, backwards.

BABBS *(in the distance)*
We've done it. We've done it all! . . . We've won!

It has been too much for Stark. She begins to wilt, her sleeves sagging. She pitches toward the sand in a despondency that is as random as her previous joy. The others continue to leap and cheer.

KESEY
We've conquered! Conquered! *(He sees Stark.)* Some the worse for wear, perhaps, but conquered never-theless.

Zonk pulls up on the motorcycle past Stark collapsed into the sand.

ZONK
I found a nice little graveyard which might be good for . . . something.

KESEY
We've got a casualty here. *(He kneels over her.)* Did you fall in exhaustion?

BABBS

I'd hate to think she didn't . . . doing all that. That'd be ungodly. Here now. My merry band of Pranksters won't be lollygagging around in the dirt! C'mon. C'mon! No, none of this misery stuff. *(He strides away, lashing the grass with a broken fishing pole like a general with a swagger stick.)* C'mon, this is the merry gang, keep 'er moving . . . this is happiness.

Stark's face rolls in the wet sand, tangled and desperate. Gretch, on the other hand, is jubilant in the river.

Hagen remains resourcefully at the camera.

HAGEN

Shittiest tripod I've ever seen . . .

STARK

However, slime, sentimental drama, plus my dear tits, you're still nothing but stuff. *(Catching sight of Cassady:)* Popeye, you dumbass shit. What are you doing running around running aground?

TRACTOR MAN *(with Kesey, Babbs and crew)* I didn't think I could do it, but I did it.

KESEY
When I saw the size of your machine, I had great faith.

As the Tractor Man and Kesey and Babbs talk, Stark rises to approach some locals who have arrived: a young mother and her redheaded baby. In the background across the river a station wagon stops. Two crewcutted men get out and lean against the fender, watching, sipping their beers.

Stark bears down upon mother and child.

TRACTOR MAN
You'll never make New York at this rate.

KESEY
That's all right. We're pretty much going out and taking what happens. That's the story.

TRACTOR MAN

Just putting it together, huh?

Stark rubs her face against the child's and coos soothing song snatches.

JANE *(voice in courtroom)*

Oh, yes . . . another thing about Stark . . . She had left her own child behind—a daughter or something.

Stark leaves the mother and child and crosses the river to the station wagon to check out the crewcuts slouched against the car. The sleeves of her drenched sweater flap crazily as she parades before them, sultry and sopping . . .

TRACTOR MAN

Well, that's a good way, but I'll tell you one thing— what makes a picture a travelogue—I don't care how interesting the picture is cause I've seen thousands of them—you got to put a little gimmick in it, a little

humor in it, something funny. Something really ridiculous because you know it gets tiresome after a while
when you start looking at scenery scenery scenery.
You got to break it up. *(He turns to leave and says
over his shoulder:)* Put a little episode of humor in it.

BABBS

Thank you.

The locals stare at the crew from the other side of the river.

HASSLER

We must be better than anything they have at home.

Back in the courtroom, Jane looks away from the KEM.

JANE

When we got to Houston this weird thing happened.
We pulled into this high-rent neighborhood to see our
friend Larry McMurtry, and he had his little boy and
he came out to the bus to greet us—not knowing what
madness was going on inside. Stark jumps out with no
clothes on and starts going for Larry's baby. I can still
see him: "Ma'am? Pardon me, ma'am? Leave him
alone. Would you take your hands off him, ma'am?"
She freaked everybody out in Houston, but she didn't
really do much damage. Larry went on to become a
famous novelist and the baby a famous rock musician.

Jane turns back to the picture on the KEM:

*Kesey, Babbs and Chuck are lounging on the Wikieup Creek
bank in the late afternoon shadows. Kesey lowers his flute.*

KESEY

Where's Cassady?

HASSLER *(appearing from left)*

I put him to sleep. You've got to rest your equipment.

Would you drive a horse into the ground? No you wouldn't.

Hagen and Stark are filming next to the creek. Hagen, none too stable himself, is trying to steady her mind.

KESEY

I hope we're picking up some of this.

CASSADY'S SPIRIT

There's her true love, Mike, intervening. Properly.

Again, the guard has to disturb her composure to glance at the evidence.

Ol' Mike had it cooled all the way; we knew that.

Neal, shirtless, comes barefooting out from the bus parked behind the trees. Jane follows closely behind. She peers over his shoulder and watches him open a pack of Camels.

NEAL

First time I's ever seduced by an Eye-talian. Or is it E? He opened a package upside down of Camels. Man, it even impressed me!

KESEY

Let's get some more of those mattresses out here and get real comfortable.

NEAL

Mattresses!

KESEY

Yes. And Cassady can regale us with tales of his railroad youth.

NEAL

Oh, god, I could do it, I suppose. I mean, what did we drive out here for, to get mosquito-bitten?

He lights up and gazes across the river.

HASSLER

It was our karma to be here, Neal. You know that.

NEAL

Oh, definitely! Right! I've never felt anything except irritation at the realities.

On the riverbank, 100 feet in front of the Pranksters, Hagen leans close to Stark and begins kissing her.

Dark green bam trees rustle in the light evening breeze. Kesey begins fluting.

HASSLER

These are artistic days that we're having. This is the only way to live.

NEAL

That's the whole thing we've been talking about. It is. Can't you freaks see it?

Sandy and Chuck light a joint, beckoning to the others. Stark, alone now, carrying her mandolin, walks toward the campsite.

STARK

There's Cassady. I knew he'd come.

Neal points across the river.

DALE

Hey! There's a stallion!

A white stallion, head cocked, stands near the water's edge on the other side of the river. George now has the flute. He begins playing.

KESEY

Oh, man! That there is a ghostly piece of animal.

Hagen turns the camera toward the horses. A brown mare has joined the white stallion.

STARK

They're liable to shoot it! A little black death.

NEAL

Oh god. Did you kill your last mother, your brother or someone? I mean, you wouldn't have cared much.

STARK

Did you ever kill someone?

NEAL

No, I didn't. I thought that the threat of course, worse than the execution, would be just enough to destroy that illusion. But I see you're held in violence.

STARK

The sun's coming up and we're—it's a gun, that's what it is.

NEAL

Better than rocks, and cuts, and glass.

STARK *(singing)*

And how longgg can it go on, how longgg can we wait for help, when no help is coming forth, and Jean-Paul Sartre is dead, oh yes . . . oh, yes; yes, that's all you must do.

NEAL

Oh, if it gets that far, you really need help. Oh, what a savior. Oh, help me, oh fart. *(He sniffs.)*

STARK

Men are always ugly.

NEAL

Really? I thought I had something.

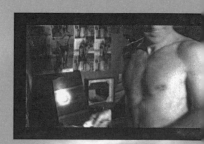

> **STARK** *(in a lovely voice)*

Well, yes.

> **NEAL**

—but it turns out to be silly.

The horses gallop past.

> **STARK**

Yes, I know. But I need to scream. *(quietly:)* I need it for the sun though. Then after the sun, a little oil. Perhaps then, maybe a little fun. No fun for us?

> **NEAL**

No, that's out entirely. Forget it.

Stark leans over and fondles Jane gratuitously. Jane, annoyed, turns to the camera and winks. Stark pretends to be not affected by the chill. She borrows Jane's cigarette, takes a drag and returns it.

> **STARK**

Oh god, this headache is getting me.

> **NEAL**

Do you have a headache?

> **STARK**

I can tell you I've got one.

> **NEAL**

I'm going to get you a few aspirins I've been saving. The last girl took fifty. It wasn't quite enough. I decided a hundred would be more like it.

> **CHEST** *(voice-over)*

And here, before you get to Houston, we see this woman going steadily crazier and we see Mister Cassady steadily having a conversation with her. Is he attempting to seduce her? Is he attempting to comfort

her? Or is he under the impression they're one and the same thing?

> JANE *(voice-over)*
> Well, I don't really know, Mr. Chest . . .

> NEAL *(rubbing tighter against Stark:)* What are we doing?

> STARK *(twanging and singing:)* I have no time to dance and sing, I have to play the fool for this king.

Neal turns from her and looks toward the bus with its waiting bunks. The setting sun throws long shadows across the campsite.

> NEAL
> Perhaps begin a more intimate level . . .

He puts his arm around Stark. She begins playing the flute.

> NEAL
> . . . and discuss the problems of flute breaking. *I* need the devil.

She laughs, and the mandolin trills. Darkness stretches over the river.

Back in the courtroom, Jane resumes her answer.

> JANE
> . . . except he *did* have this quality of driving a lot of people crazy. He would tap into your head and start telling you what you were thinking. He could be very accurate but he could also get you thinking about what he said you were thinking. And that could be very disturbing.

> CHEST
> Couldn't he tell he was disturbing some people?

JANE

He had a sadistic side to him, I'm sure he did. But he was never sadistic to me.

CHEST

How were you lucky enough to escape the sadistic side?

JANE

I wasn't that easy a prey. I don't like to let my trips go outside my own plans, especially when I'm pregnant.

CHEST

Then, Jane, why didn't you have misgivings about the chemicals which you were ingesting during this time?

JANE

It wasn't till after Emily was born that I heard that LSD supposedly was terrible for the young embryo. I didn't know at the time. I mean as far as I was concerned, acid was a great drug. It was obviously a good

drug. It never occurred to me that it would be bad for the baby, no.

CHEST

Did you later think that perhaps it might have been bad for her?

Jane looks away from Chest and smiles into the courtroom audience at her pretty daughter. Emmy is holding a bright-eyed red-haired baby. Emmy smiles and waves the baby's hand at Jane.

JANE

It was very clear to me from the day she was born that she was a fine, bright, healthy, intelligent human, just like my little grandson there.

CHEST

Having apparently spent quite a bit of the time preceding the birth under the effect of mind-altering chemicals, how can one be so confident of clarity—?

JANE

You're acting very rude, Mister Chest.

CHEST

I feel it's the responsibility of those present at this hearing to understand exactly what happened.

JANE

Rudeness will get you nowhere.

CHEST

You realize the absence of your response will be conspicuous on the transcripts.

JANE

Take it to the judge.

TOOEY *(interrupting)*

Quite so, Mister Chest. Miss Burton's not on trial here, nor is her credibility. I must object.

The bailiff rises to glance over his podium at the bus and its V-meter. The needles jump. His gavel bangs.

BAILIFF

Sustained.

CHEST

Very well. Back to your clear opinion of Mr. Cassady, Miss Burton. How do you explain your—ah—unimpressed view of the defendant in the light of Mister John Page Browning's contrary vision of him as an inspiration?

Jane leans her chin on her hand and gazes at the KEM. It is producing shots of Neal struggling burlesquely uphill under the burden of a huge wooden cross.

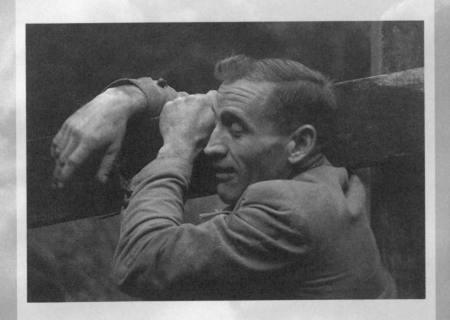

JANE *(voice-over)*

A lot of people consider him a great inspiration. He said himself that he was a Christ person. More loaves-and-fishes fantasy, I imagine. "I tripped for your sins," and all that.

CHEST *(voice-over)*

That's fascinating. Did others see him in this light?

JANE *(voice-over)*

Some other *men* maybe. A lot of this great love for Cassady was this male trip. I don't know how many women you're going to find who saw him as a Christ person. I think he must've represented some kind of individualism that seemed real far out from that masculine point of view.

JANE *(in courtroom)*

You know, individualism is a deadly thing! in *what*-ever form. I believe in the social revolution. This mighty, individualistic "Lone Cry to the Heavens!"—that's not the way. Because you can't make your fucking lone cry to the heavens without approximately 50,000 people making your food, your house, your clothes, your car, your gasoline, your everything.

But now I'm tripping . . . back to Neal. He knew he was fucked up; that's the sad part of it. Too macho, too macho. What he was, was the real smart Catholic boy who got sucked up to by Kerouac. If he'd been left to be a drunken Irish worker/Catholic, he would have had a wife and a bunch of kids and beat 'em up a lot and he would have had that. But he got in with some poets and he got aspirations, so then he was split between the two worlds . . . but there was never any decent world for him to start with. Really. These macho Irish Catholic wild dudes have no chance. You know why?

Chest has been watching the KEM pictures of Cassady strutting shirtless, sinewy and brazen as a banty across the American landscape. He starts from his reverie to answer.

CHEST

No . . . why?

JANE

Because of people like me, hee hee hee.

The KEM pictures hold, stopping the three images in midstrut. Chest blinks. Tooey and Jane exchange smiles. The fan whirs overhead, desultory and useless, as Jane leaves the stand.

The bus, superimposed over the map, travels down the desert highway. Inside the bus, young Zonk sleeps, bearded mouth open, head lolling from side to side with the bus's swerving.

BAILIFF *(voice-over)*

And you?

ZONK *(voice-over)*

Zonk.

The bailiff pauses, gavel held lifted.

BAILIFF

Zonk?

ZONK

Or Zonker. Or Steve Lambrecht of San Jose.

BAILIFF *(rapping gavel)*

Be seated.

CHEST *(reading)*

San Jose, California?

ZONK

Where I live in my tasteful suburban home and manage
my simple middleclass business with my two suburban
sons.

CHEST

If you please, ah Zonk . . . *(handing him the pointer)*
I've always been dreadful at geography. We were driving through?

*The KEM continues moving the bus south. Zonk watches the
pictures but makes no attempt to point out the bus's position.
He turns instead to confront Chest.*

ZONK

Mister Chest, you are aware that I am a hostile witness.

CHEST

I hope to discover no hostility, Zonk. I'm simply trying
to get at the truth . . . about this tangled path, and
this unfortunate soul's part in it; his influence, et
cetera.

Chest's voice trails off. Something else across the room has caught his attention. The attendant Tooey sent to the Rosebud Room is returning with a rose-colored note. Tooey starts reading it.

CHEST
. . . so if you would kindly lead our attention further along said path, the court would be most grateful.

But Chest's mind is on Tooey and her note. Zonk begins to point on the map, intoning routes and towns as the KEM responds with pertinent pictures. Chest, however, turns his back on it and strolls innocently toward Tooey's table.

ZONK *(voice-over)*
We slept the night at Wikieup. Then the next morning headed out, down 93 . . .

The pointer points. The bus roars and rolls across the desert, Cassady at the wheel. A tinny transistorized livestock report tries to penetrate the roar and the static. Cassady turns and reaches a gloved hand back to adjust the dial of a little radio dangling from an interior light behind his driver's seat.

RADIO

Hog prices took a fall this morning in Prescott but don't you folks out there fret. Hogs always—Zeek!—Zeek!—"I'll pick up a ten-spot in Prescott I know, A-riding a bronc at the big rodeo."

Tooey looks up from her note in time to see Chest picking up her cup of whiskey. She folds the paper and puts it on the desk under her pen stand. Chest ignores her and seats himself on her desk and sips.

CHEST

Enjoying the bus ride, Defender Tooey?

She doesn't answer. She leans forward instead so she can see the KEM around his bulk. The bus is rolling through the night.

ZONK *(voice-over)*

You go through a lot of pretty country . . . Wickenburg . . . Beardsley . . . El Mirage . . .

Inside the bus Cassady's gloved hand is moving from task to task: the gear, the throttle, Stark's leg, the radio . . .

RADIO

". . . and the Good Lord knows the reason I'm just a cowpoke."—Zeet!—"By the time I get to Phoenix . . . she'll be rising . . ."

Stark, seated beside Neal, watches with hollowed eyes the desert rolling past.

ZONK *(voice-over)*

By the time we got to Phoenix she was still rising . . .

The parked bus is spraycan-lettered A VOTE FOR BARRY IS A VOTE FOR FUN. The lettering finished, flags fly from every window

AKRY IS A VOTE FOR FUN

and Cassady pulls away from the curb and drives away down the Phoenix mainstreet, backwards.

> **CHEST** *(voice-over)*
> Who, Zonk, was still rising?

> **ZONK** *(voice-over)*
> Stark. That's what this is all getting to, isn't it, Mister Chest? Stark Naked?

> **CHEST** *(voice-over)*
> If you say so, Zonk. Though she still seems to be decently covered.

> **ZONK** *(voice-over)*
> Yeah, well she didn't really start letting it all hang out until we hit Texas, and the sun went down.

The setting sun shows the DALLAS CITY LIMITS *sign out the bus window. Cassady's hand reaches for the radio.*

> **RADIO**
> Zeekle! "Big dee little aye double ell aye, big dee little aye double ell aye, big dee little aye double ell aye esss!"

The city looms into the windshield. On the top of the bus Chuck points up to the ominous brick side of the Dallas Book Depository.

At the wheel below Cassady advises the city:

> **CASSADY**
> A vote for Barry is a vote for fun!

Then they are out of town. From the top of the bus the dark desert road swoops off into the distance. The desert dawn wheels overhead and the wind rushes by. A diesel passes, baying forlornly. Cassady's gloved hand fishes for music:

RADIO

Zeek!—Squawk!—"Abilene . . . Abilene . . . Prettiest town I ever seen. . . . Nobody'll ever treat you mean . . . in Abilene. . . ."

ZONK *(voice-over)*

By dawn she was down to her panties. I was on top of the bus with Chuck, trying to get some rest, so I didn't see her. . . . But I knew something was up.

A truck comes booming up on the bus, starts to pass, then abruptly gears down and tails in close. The driver gawks, leaning near the windshield. Another truck approaches and also gears down.

Back in the courtroom, Chest is still sitting on Tooey's desk, sipping her drink. They are both intrigued by the footage roaring out of the KEM across the room.

CHEST

You sensed something unusual was taking place in the bus below?

ZONK *(voice-over)*

No. On the back platform. Apparently Stark had crawled out the rear window, over the motorcycle.

CHEST

Didn't any of the other riders perceive what was happening?

ZONK

They got the idea eventually.

From the top of the bus Chuck and Zonk look back at a long line of trucks following in the dawn, jockeying in and out for a peek at the treat on the bus's rear platform. There is a shout and a curse from below.

> ZONK *(voice-over)*

That must have been when Kesey told her to get her shapely ass back on board.

Inside, the passengers watch a woman come crawling through the bus's rear window. The sweeping headlights of the trucks silhouette her bare breasts. Laughing, Stark charges up the aisle, straight into the windshield; the glass spiders out from her forehead.

Far out. I'd forgotten how we got that broken windshield.

On the top of the bus, Zonk and Chuck watch the nose of the bus ease off the highway, onto the gently dipping shoulder. The rising sun lights a carpet of tiny purple flowers. The bus stops. There is more yelling from below. Then Stark appears. She leaps out the bus door and runs laughing onto the flowering roadside carpet. Her black panties emphasize her fleeing posterior.

> ZONK *(voice-over)*

Yes, a pretty little butt, it was.

She slows in her wild run. Her laughter turns to yelps. She suddenly gives up and flops down in despair, weeping in the treacherous weeds.

> ZONK *(voice-over)*

. . . out into the goatheads, raving in thorny despair . . .

Chest turns from the KEM and looks warily at Zonk.

> CHEST

Goatheads?

> ZONK

Stickers that look like the head of a goat. She had run out not only bareback but barefoot to boot; all that way into the thorns before she realized it.

Chest has left Tooey's table and is walking back toward the witness chair, smiling to himself as he palms her report.

> CHEST
>
> Did no one attempt to aid the poor lady?

> ZONK
>
> We carried her back on board and picked the goat-heads off her.

> CHEST
>
> Mister Cassady helped as well?

> ZONK
>
> He was driving. Look, I know what you're trying to show with this line of questioning, but I don't think it's fair to fix this on Cassady. He didn't have any more influence on her than anyone else.

> CHEST
>
> Very well, Zonk. I'll discontinue this line of questioning for the moment. Let us see what kind of influence Mister Cassady had on persons other than poor Miss Naked. How did he first come to your attention?

> ZONK
>
> I was a young kid, maybe 13 years old . . .

The KEM produces a picture of skinny 13-year-old Steve Lambrecht showing off for an 8mm family camera. He is tightroping across the top of a sign, TIRES RECAPPED RETREADED. *Beyond the teetering boy's legs out of focus in the shopyard next door, a shirtless man tosses tires in the afternoon heat.*

> ZONK *(voice-over)*
>
> . . . my dad had the White Truck franchise in San Jose and there was this truck tire repair place next door.

The KEM enlarges the shirtless man, slows him. The grainy image drifts through the heat waves in a dreamy adagio with the huge truck tire.

Also this muscley little tire changer who was just absolutely amazing to watch.

On the KEM the 13-year-old boy squints into the afternoon sun, the same awe in his face as in Zonk's voice as he watches the tire changer.

> CHEST *(voice-over)*
>
> Did he speak to you?

> ZONK *(voice-over)*
>
> Not until years later, when I started hanging around those parties around Stanford . . . and La Honda.

> CHEST
>
> To get on the bus?

> ZONK
>
> I wasn't interested in being straight all my life.

On the bus Zonk cavorts furiously, slows suddenly and sleeps deeply. The sleeping frame holds and he looks dead.

> CHEST *(voice-over)*
>
> And you calculated that Mister Cassady could be helpful in giving your existence a few twists and turns if you tagged along. Would you say you were enamored of him?

> ZONK *(voice-over)*
>
> Yes, I was enamored of him. He was joyous. He could take social and emotional and cosmic changes just like he could take ninety-degree corners . . . on four wheels or two. My god, didn't you ever read *On the Road*? He was a living legend!

CHEST

A most influential role model?

ZONK

Yes.

CHEST

The same kind of example you would not object to influencing, say, the lives of your two wonderful suburban sons?

ZONK

Yes, in a symbolic way, yes I—

CHEST

Even though this man—

He holds up a sheet of rose-colored paper. Tooey looks beneath the pen holder on her desk. The report is gone. She glares at Chest.

—this absolutely amazing example with the many aliases *(reading)* . . . "came to an apparent willful end, alone, on a remote stretch of railroad tracks in a foreign land, his system filled with such an abundance of intoxicating substances that it was impossible for him to find shelter. . . ."*(He lowers the report and confronts Zonk.)* In short, *froze* himself to death! With a perverseness that was, if not blatantly *in*, at the very last was bordering *on*, the suicidal, wouldn't you say, Zonk? Wouldn't you?

Tooey, seething, stands to appeal to the bailiff.

TOOEY

I strongly object! The opposer has not only been leading the witness, he has been leading him with data purloined from the defense's desk! I ask that both this

tactic as well as this witness be relinquished immediately.

BAILIFF

Objection?

The V-meter registers, just barely, SUSTAINED. The gavel bangs.

Witness may step down.

As Zonk leaves the stand, Chest walks back to Tooey's table. He is skimming through the remainder of her report.

CHEST

No record of last words, though, Miss Tooey.

TOOEY

Skunk.

CHEST

Pity. It's hard to have a good living legend die without a couple of legendary last words.

Finished with the report, Chest tosses it on Tooey's desk and turns, preparing to sit on the desk edge again. Tooey slides the pen holder, spikelike, under him, daring him to try.

TOOEY

Were I the honorable opposer I'd be careful where I parked that from here on.

Chest remains standing, but continues to whisper:

CHEST

I doubt, though, that anything he might have said at his passing could have helped his case any more than the rubbish he reeled out preceding it. Paula Sundsten, please . . .

BAILIFF

Paula Sundsten to the stand.

Chest leaves to take on his new witness. Tooey turns to her assistant:

TOOEY

Try again, honey, would you please? Try under L . . . ?

ASSISTANT

Under "Last Words," Miss Tooey? I already checked . . .

TOOEY

Try under "Legendary."

The assistant leaves. Tooey sees a sharp-featured woman sitting regally on the stand, already answering Chest.

GRETCH

No. Gretch. Not Paula. Not Sundsten, not Miss, Mrs., Miz or Mam'zelle. Gretch.

CHEST

Just Gretch?

GRETCH

. . . the Wretch.

CHEST

Very well, Gretch. If we might continue where our friend Zonk left off . . . into the subject of the final disposition of the girl called Kathy alias Stark Naked—

GRETCH

You mean Stark's dead too?

CHEST

Dead?

GRETCH

You said "final disposition . . . ?"

CHEST

I meant it only within the scope of this inquiry. But, as a matter of fact, there's been no response to our summons. . . . However, to the question I was endeavoring to ask—

GRETCH

Mister, you've got to ask me short questions. My mind's moving too fast for long ones.

CHEST

What happened to Stark after you got to Houston?

GRETCH

Jane told you what Stark did.

CHEST

But I'm still curious as to what led up to it. If, perhaps, you could recapitulate . . .

GRETCH

Oh brother.

CHEST

Well, what comes to mind that seems significant? About Stark. How would you say she appeared?

GRETCH

Not too stable.

CHEST

And would you say her stability quotient increased or decreased during the brief period you observed her?

GRETCH

Listen, she was a source of comedy from the second she stepped on the bus.

CHEST

Why do you say that?

GRETCH

Because she had a lot of out-of-phase reactions to things.

CHEST

Like what, Gretch?

GRETCH

Like getting one lobster tail to feed twelve hungry Pranksters. You'd have to say that was a little ridiculous, wouldn't you?

CHEST

A culinary *faux pas* of the first water, I will grant; but all I am trying to ascertain is the effect of these incidents on Miss . . . ahh Naked's condition during that period.

GRETCH

Short questions.

CHEST

Was this woman crazier when she got off this damned bus than when she got on!?

GRETCH

She was crazier when she got off; that I *would* have to say.

CHEST

That is *all* I wanted to know. Thank you.

Gretch starts to get up but Tooey rises and approaches the witness chair, stopping her.

TOOEY

If I may use a portion of the opposition's arena?

CHEST

By all means.

TOOEY

Gretch, I was struck by a comment Jane made during her testimony concerning you and Mr.—?

GRETCH

Babbs.

TOOEY

Something about "the greatest acid high in the history of the world"?

GRETCH

Yeah, at Wikieup.

The KEM is rerunning Gretch-in-the-pond at Wikieup. Tooey and Gretch-in-the-courtroom watch.

TOOEY

And you had taken whatever Stark had taken?

GRETCH

When I saw the dent she'd made in the lemonade I got my share, if that's what you mean . . .

TOOEY

Yet you seemed to have been having a fine time here. Was it just because you "fell in love" as Jane said?

Gretch-in-the-pond is slowed down as she approaches her moment of agony/ecstasy.

GRETCH *(voice-over)*

Sure, sure. Falling in love is fun. But it was more than that. You see, Stark aspired to be this actress, always coming on a little stagey. Unnatural, you know? . . .

afraid she was going to get something *on* her, so when it started getting like it does on acid—*slimy*—she started getting freaky.

CHEST *(interrupting)*
Whereas you were elected, if I remember correctly, Slime Queen.

GRETCH
I figured, once you're in it, you're in it. And everything opened itself up to me.

The face in the pond dissolves through emotion after emotion— rage, hysteria, misery, fear—then looks at something in her hand. Her hand has brought up a gob of green algae. She holds it aloft and peers into it. The sun glistens on a drop and the glisten divides and divides again and is a suddenly proliferating mandala of pond life.

GRETCH (*voice-over*)

I felt like the nature spirits and stuff in there were saying, "Hey! We're finally in contact with human beings! Hey, you guys; do you have any idea how long we've been trying to get through to you?!" Anyway, I decided: "Go ahead, shake hands with 'em." And there was no more murkiness. It was super-clean, crystalline.

The slowly gyrating pond droplet darkens. The magnified creatures recede, becoming pinpoints of light, stars in the sky.

TOOEY (*voice-over*)

Then in your opinion, Gretch, Stark's going crazier stemmed from her being in some way out of touch with nature *before* this trip started.

GRETCH (*voice-over*)

In my opinion, yes.

TOOEY (*voice-over*)

Thank you, Gretch.

One of the stars swells into a swirling emerald sun that blots out the heavens. The green haze comes into focus. It is the algae. Then we are back in the courtroom.

This time Chest intervenes.

CHEST

Another moment, Gretch. I think I *would* like you to go ahead and recount for us what went on after your arrival in Houston.

GRETCH

Oh, all right. As Jane said, when we got to Larry's she came out of the bus—actually she was wearing a blanket; we'd wrapped her in this blanket after the goatheads—and as she threw open her arms, to greet

Larry and the little kid . . . she became—ta *da!*—
Stark Naked.

CHEST

And then?

GRETCH

We got her in the house, wrapped her back up in the
blanket . . . but, somehow during the day—she slipped
away. We looked for her. Not *all* the time . . .

*Chest is watching the KEM roll pictures of the gang frolicking
around a swimming pool in the Texas afternoon. There is care-
less, casual laughter and the clink of glasses.*

CHEST

Didn't you in fact spend *most* of the time cavorting at
your friend's swimming pool?

GRETCH

He'd asked for help painting his patio wall. We decided
to pitch in while he was at work.

*The wall is being painted in the same meandering organic style
of the bus. Cassady, forsaking the joys of painting for the lit-
erary, basks in the poolside sun reading a book.*

GRETCH *(voice-over)*

Neal begged off anything to do with painting. He was
color blind—

CASSADY'S SPIRIT

. . . grass looked red and I was so mad at that darned
grass I took up driving.

GRETCH

—so his job that afternoon was the backboard. For
the waterball game.

Cassady performs another of his adagio spectaculars, this time with a board. He almost uses it, almost loses it into the pool, almost dances with it, almost drives a nail in it. . . . The patio in the background fills with color; everyone finally leaps laughing into the pool.

CHEST
And this is how you passed the agonizing vigil during your hapless comrade's absence?

GRETCH
We also did the laundry.

Hanging out around Larry's house. Dale reads nervously. Larry paces. In irritation, Gretch throws laundry about. Through the shadowy residential streets of Houston, Stark strolls, wrapped in a blanket.

A phone rings. Kesey picks it up.

GRETCH *(voice-over)*
By the time we found her it was too late.

Houston streets, shot from the top of the bus. Bouncing and driving. The bouncing stops. Larry gets out and heads toward the steps of the Houston Arraignment Facility Center for Undetermined Cases. At the top of the steps he is joined by a policeman who pushes the buzzer. A doctor in a white smock steps out and immediately begins berating Larry. No words can be heard. But he points to a window above and all look: a woman's form can be seen behind the slats of a venetian blind. The form pulls down a section of slats to reveal for a moment her nakedness, then she is grasped from each side by uniformed matrons who drag her away. The blinds snap closed.

Larry looks back down to find the doctor and the policeman eyeing him suspiciously. Too late he realizes that he is also in hot water in Houston, and they are ushering him toward the door. He tries to protest, looking over his shoulder to the bus for some hope of rescue. But the engine ignites with a roar. The image begins to bounce again. Cassady hollers, "Boo-ard!" and the bus starts moving to leave the captured Stark and her rescuer. Chest is aghast.

> CHEST
>
> You left them *both? both* abandoned to the chewing maw of chance?—and not a very good one, at that—

> GRETCH
>
> We had to roll.

> CHEST
>
> Meaning, especially, wouldn't you have to say, Mister Cassady had to roll?

> TOOEY
>
> Never mind, Gretch. Enough. I thank you.

> CHEST
>
> And I you, Miss Tooey, for the light you have helped throw on this dim business. Now, if it please the court . . .

The KEM reverses, speeding back to the scene at the top of the hospital steps. The face of the doctor holds, close up.

> CHEST *(voice-over)*
>
> . . . the opposition would like to call, as our case's last witness, a member of this fiasco who was *never* on the bus.

The face cuts to the next witness. It's the same doctor, 25 years older, looking prosperous and important. He completes Chest's statement:

DOCTOR

—nor would never *hope* to be, may I emphatically reiterate. It was sick. I hate to be harsh but that was my diagnosis. Sick!

TOOEY

Is that a harsh diagnosis, Doctor, or a harsh judgment?

DOCTOR

A judgment, madam. Mine. I had an opportunity to judge firsthand some of the exotic effects of the "being on the bus" business.

CHEST

When you were Doctor in charge of admissions at—

DOCTOR

Houston Arraignment Facility Center for Undetermined Cases. We called it HAVE-KOOK. After seven years in that Texas cockroach castle, I was, I think, madam, qualified to make some judgments, even some harsh ones. *(Neck stretching, Doctor Richy turns to address the whole courtroom):* I was so struck by this case that I have devoted myself to the syndrome ever since. With the possible exception of Hollister in California and Sandoz in Switzerland, I think I can say, without exaggerating, that I am the foremost authority.

One of the court audience sniffs loudly at the statement. It is Doctor Knot (Babbs), sitting rigidly in an officer's uniform festooned with medical corps insignia. He frowns severely at Dr. Richy's expert opinions.

CHEST

This syndrome? In terms of our patient? You would describe it as?

DOCTOR

I have come to call her condition *psychochemillogical breakdown*. A person is first chemically disarmed and dis-armored, then bombarded psychologically. From the time of this historic incarceration to the present, I have personally seen literally thousands of similar cases. Over a hundred at *one time* after the famous Rolling Stones concert at Altamont. Over a hundred! Psychochemillogically-broken zombies! Or, if you will, "burn-outs."

CHEST

Can they be helped?

DOCTOR

Some can. With time, and understanding, and modern consciousness modification techniques, but some simply can not be reached. They are, as they say on the street, simply, "around that corner."

CHEST

And it takes the two traumas to perpetrate this outrage? Violations on both chemical and personal fronts? Intentionally? Monstrous. Whyever, Doctor, do you think one civilized human should have the impulse to do this evil thing to another?

DOCTOR

Who can say? The evil impetus is out of my field. Why did Manson weaken and warp unwary young minds? Why did Hitler put amphetamines in the water supply at his early rallies? Psychopathic "power trip," most probably. Who can say? Perhaps that is what the evil impulse; at its core, it always is—

Dr. Richy's diatribe has provoked the rival doctor in the gallery to scribble an incensed note on his prescription pad. He folds

it so his embossed name shows: Doctor Captain Knot. He hisses to one of the attendants to come near and hands him the note, pointing to Tooey at the front of the courtroom.

Tooey is tilted back in her chair, listening glumly to Doctor Richy. The attendant's hand comes into view with the folded note. Tooey opens it and reads as Doctor Richy winds up his testimony.

—a power trip; no more no less.

The accused spirit jumps and giggles. The guard scowls at him.

CASSADY'S SPIRIT
Dear me, you got me all mixed up with another fellow, hee hee ho. I just came to sit in this park.

CHEST
Thank you, Doctor Richy. The opposition rests its case.

TOOEY *(without looking up from the note:)* Rests what case? The opposition hasn't even leveled charges, let alone argued them. Mr. Cassady can't be found guilty of *nothing*, Mr. Chest.

CHEST
Of nothing? Very well then, would you settle for charges of *(looking first to Roy and Chloe)* . . . of social terrorism? *(then to Page)* flagrant false propheteering? *(to Zonk)* primrose pathing in the worse degree? *(to John and then Jane)* monomania, sexism, racism, escapism, and finally *(to Dr. Richy)* psychochem—psychic rape! Miss Tooey, with all due consideration for your gastrics, it is not the duty of this court to quibble over parking tickets and check bouncing! We both know there is only one charge. Now, we've

heard the witnesses. Are we going to answer the testimonies or not?

TOOEY

Doctor Richy, if you would yield the chair a while, I would like to call Dr. Knot.

Babbs (Dr. Knot) rises and approaches the stand, stately and impressive.

Doctor Richy gives him a puzzled scowl as they pass each other. Doctor Knot looks neither left nor right, but mutters in passing: "Foremost authority, my foot." He takes the stand and raises his hand, at attention.

BAILIFF

How would you be called?

KNOT

Doctor . . . or Knot . . . Knot, doctor of medicine.

BAILIFF

Would you take a seat?

TOOEY

Dr. Knot, as nearly as I can make out *(holding up prescription)*, you take a quite vehement opposition to Doctor Richy's expert opinions.

KNOT

He's no more a recognized authority than I'm not a doctor. From one passing incident and a few well-placed papers Richy becomes the foremost authority? Hardly. With your permission, Richy is a joke in the field. Sure he's treated thousands of burn-outs. He's still treating them. He can't reach them because he never really knew where they were at. He hasn't made human contact since he left Houston and opened up

his famous clinic in California. Too bad he *didn't* get on the bus. It couldn't have hurt.

TOOEY
I take it you were, Doctor Knot . . . on the bus?

KNOT
Yes, I can tell you I was on it! And it was no bed of roses . . . miserable conditions, the most primitive of tools . . . ages before I even got a space for my infirmary. I had to operate in whatever back-of-the-bus nook I might find.

On the KEM the bus is rolling. Inside, Babbs has discovered a festering wound on Hagen's leg and is cleaning it with gin. He takes a drink, swishes it around his mouth and spits it into the open sore. Hagen writhes. Babbs hands him the gin to sedate him.

Tooey, looking on, realizes she may have called the wrong witness.

KNOT *(voice-over)*
. . . make-do antiseptics . . .

Babbs sticks a tampon into the open wound, tapes it fast, then lights the little white string. Chest is delighted.

CHEST
A *brilliant* make-do, Doctor; cauterization and all.

KNOT
Thank you. I thought so.

CHEST
It is the customary practice at an inquiry of this nature to ask a professional witness to establish his credentials.

TOOEY

Yes, please, Doctor. Where did you receive the bulk
of your training?

KNOT

In the United States Marine Corps.

TOOEY

You were a doctor in the Marines?

KNOT

No, a pilot.

*He pulls a batch of cards out of his billfold and begins flipping
through them.*

Here's my flying license: proves I have no fear of
flights, can therefore function in atmospheres where
ordinary doctors cannot.

Chest apathetically examines the card. Tooey waits.

My instrument card: allows me to handle instruments with calm aplomb.

TOOEY *(confused)*

Do you intend not to distinguish yourself from a professional doctor? I mean, you are a licensed doctor are you not, Doctor Knot?

KNOT

I eschewed medical school in favor of the richer colleges of manifold experiences.

TOOEY

You didn't acquire *any* medical license? How do you call yourself a doctor?

KNOT

That's my name. My first name is Doctor, my second name is Captain, my last name is Knot.

TOOEY

Your *name* is Doctor? I'm most appreciative of your generosity in wishing to share your wisdom with this court but as it turns out I don't—

CHEST

Miss Tooey, as long as this Mister Doctor Knot has agreed to share his wisdom, why don't we take advantage of his professional expertise, whatever it is, or is not?

TOOEY

Help yourself, Chest.

KNOT

Here's my Red Cross life-saving card: license to not practice in liquids if the case needs be. First Aid card: for cases not serious. My High Explosives Handlers card.

Chest has been examining each card with mock attention; he starts at this last one.

CHEST

High Explosives?

KNOT

Sometimes with extremely tough virulent strains it's necessary to blast.

CHEST *(noting some knowing laughs from the gallery:)* Not being among the initiates, I'm afraid I'll have to ask you to elucidate, Doctor. Specifically, how does this apply to the use of these drugs and this bus trip?

KNOT *(after thinking hard)* An awful disease had crept into our American society—insidiously, steadily, in the thirty or so years since the war, practically unchecked. By the mid-sixties everyone who wasn't wearing blinders because

of vested interests, like our "foremost authority" out there, knew that the epidemic had nearly reached Condition Terminal.

Chest raises his hand.

> **CHEST**
> I think that's enough. You may step down.

> **TOOEY** *(getting up)*
> Just a minute, Doctor Knot. A disease that affected whom? In what ways?

> **KNOT** *(voice-over)*
> Everyone was susceptible. Still is. This viral condition infects the cells of society and overrides natural functions. The condition is revealed by a growing complacency with the ethical direction of the state, a hardening of the heart which finally spreads to render the victim's perceptive senses paralyzed, so that the only sights, sounds and ideas that can be accepted by the person are those already prescreened and marked permissible.

> **CHEST** *(voice-over)*
> This is rather obscure . . .

> **KNOT** *(rushing on, under a full head of steam:)* Thought patterns repeated over and over form a mental screen located in the frontal lobe—sometimes right side; sometimes left. Once formed, the screen becomes impenetrable. The disease spreads until the entity has lost all its powers of spontaneity. This mental net was suffocating our sovereign states in 1964. Our country was dying!

> **CHEST** *(voice-over)*
> Come now, it couldn't have been all that serious, Mr. Doctor.

KNOT *(voice-over)*

Serious! It almost took over *entirely* . . . waged war;
fostered fear; elected its own damn *president* was how
serious it became! The infection had gained a strong-
hold in the plumpest parts of the American spirit. The
situation was *bound* to become—still *might* become—
terminal, unless that cancerous screen is blasted away,
like scales from the eye, tartar from the tooth—obli-
terated!—so the healthy new impressions are allowed
to pour in.

TOOEY

Does the disease have a name?

KNOT

Fatheadedness. Luckily, since every coin has two
sides, the presence of Fatheadedness also implied a
cure. By 1964 some reputed antitoxins had been per-
fected and were circulating in certain nonprofessional
areas. Our lack of expertise certainly qualified us, and
we were granted a sizeable requisition for our journey.

*On all three screens the big gallon of orange-colored juice is
being tipped up for drinking, as the bus bounces, as the bus
sits, as the sun goes down and comes up.*

We ourselves were not immune to the disease so nat-
urally we too needed the antitoxin.

CHEST *(rising to his feet)*

Miss Tooey, ask Doctor Knot what he thinks the effect
of this antitoxin as he calls it would be on someone of
unstable mental fiber.

*The KEM provides the records of Stark's agonized face in the
sand, rising to look at something horrible impending.*

TOOEY *(voice-over)*

I'd like to know the answer to that myself. Go ahead, Doctor Knot, answer him.

The white horse appears, huge and near. His teeth and hooves are dripping blood. He rears, pawing at Stark's face. A crimson river pours over her.

KNOT *(voice-over)*

When the habit-screen is removed there is often a time of panic when everything familiar seems suddenly to be gone, or going. The terrified ego tries to abandon ship. If the person isn't assisted through this trauma, he might do something that attracts the attention of the institutional watchdogs and end up in the hands of people like Doctor Richy. This outcome invariably prolongs the torment.

The red turns orange and the jug of juice is lowered to reveal the nondoctor performing another mad operation in the back of the bus.

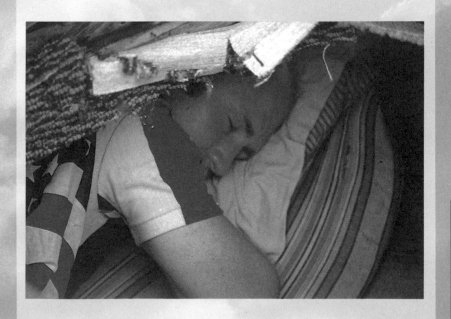

KNOT *(voice-over)*

Your everyday problems, these, though . . . mishaps
. . . cuts; sores; bruises suffered in the rigors. Gad!
you can see the conditions . . . !

*In his back-of-the-bus hospital the nondoctor is stalking a par-
ticularly spectacular case. A great dark hulk with four arms,
and hands for feet, has wandered in seeking aid. The doctor
pounces on the specimen, wrestles it to submission and holds it
while Kesey loads a huge syringe with orange juice. After in-
jecting this potion into the creature, Dr. Knot packs the wound
with a charge and once again lights the fuse. The hulk begins
to quake, then explodes and topples to the floor. Its head rolls
off. It is an empty gallon jug. In the courtroom Knot smiles
proudly at the operation.*

KNOT

Yep. Sometimes had to blast.

TOOEY *(tearing her eyes from
the KEM:)* Thank you Doctor Knot; you've been more
helpful than I—more than helpful.

*She dismisses Dr. Knot and starts with her notes, uncertain
where to go next with her case. Knot has left the witness stand
and is returning to the pews, past Chest.*

CHEST *(An aside, as Knot did
to Dr. Richy:)* Ship's Doctor my foot. I wonder you
didn't sport a bus chaplain, as well.

KNOT

We did.

TOOEY *(looking up from her
notes, hopefully:)* Oh?

KNOT

Certainly. Perhaps not officially ordained but nevertheless most highly charged.

TOOEY

Highly Charged?

BAILIFF *(calling)*

Highly Charged to the stand!

DALE *(taking witness chair:)*

Just Dale. Dale Kesey. Highly Charged I've not been called since the bus trip.

TOOEY

One of the Kesey brothers?

DALE

Cousins. And I wasn't any bus chaplain. I don't know what that fool doctor was talking about. I mean, I have done some preaching now and then; some witnessing . . .

TOOEY

Might we say, then, that you were of a spiritual bent?

DALE

I suppose . . . but no more than I was bent in other ways. Musically, say.

TOOEY

I noticed your instrument case. A violinist?

DALE

No. More a fiddler bower.

TOOEY

Spiritually bent and fiddle-bowed. Dale, Ms. Burton mentioned something else. Ah, could you tell us *(she flips through her notepad after a phrase)* what is a "WASP"?

DALE

White Anglo-Saxon Protestant. That's what we were when we started. West Coast WASPs.

TOOEY

And when you got to the East Coast . . . ?

DALE

First, we had all that South to go through . . .

Dale takes up the pointer from beside his chair. The tip searches about the South for where the trip left off in Texas.

DALE *(voice-over)*

Usually you don't go to New York from California by way of Florida.

The pointer finds its place, strikes the map, the bus roars, rocks. Cassady's gloved hand guiding it down a leafy tunnel of southern streets . . .

But I have since thought maybe it was more than Cassady's hand on the wheel.

The radio: "Walp, now, the purple's on the sage and the coffee's on the stove down here't Pete's Pecan Palace, folks—" The gloved fingers find the dial. Zeek! *"—rose, mah rose of San An—"* Zeek. *"—her eyes are bright as diamonds, they sparkle like the dew . . ."*

DALE *(voice-over, still musing from courtroom)* Maybe it was meant, so's this wagonload of WASPs could sop up a little soul.

CHEST
Hold everything! This celebration of this venture's holy purpose is frankly making me a little *queasy!* Dale, did you ever actually witness any kind of manifestation—oil poured from the sky? fire from the earth? the bestowal of a bright gold halo on Mr. Cassady, or Mr. Kesey, or any of the rest of you potential prophets?

DALE
Not exactly.

CHEST
Did this journey to the east ever pause to pay its respects to a church? A seminary? *Any* holy place?

DALE
We did go pay our respects at IFIF.

CHEST
IFIF?

DALE
At Millbrook, Leary and Alpert's scene. The International Federation for Internal Freedom.

ALL PERSONS ARE HEREBY

FORBIDDEN

TO FISH, TRAP OR SHOOT ON
THESE PREMISES

TRESPASS

HEREON

Hancock Cattle Corp

PRIVATE
PROPERTY
NO PARKING
AT ANY TIME

The bus is allowed through a huge stone wall by a drawgate. It winds in low gear down a vast, oak-shaded estate, fluting and jabbering. The spirit finds all this very exciting.

CASSADY'S SPIRIT
Here comes Ginsberg off the back of the bus at IFIF. Ah, hear the music. Open up!

The guard's eyes go wide in response to an unseen goose from the docket behind her.

DALE *(voice-over)*
Millbrook was the high-rent counterpart to the bus. A lovely old mansion to quarter the services . . . Which were ministered by doctors and professors and lovely young heiresses. The well-heeled works. Look; that's Ginsberg out on troll patrol . . .

In the courtroom, Allen Ginsberg and Peter Orlovsky sit near each other on a pew, watching the ancient footage. Gregorian chants and birds sing in the distance.

ALLEN

Look Peter, there's me sweeping up broken glass . . .

PETER

It was a pretty day . . . very green.

Green indeed. The mansion, which could be glimpsed for a moment through the trees, is becoming shrouded in green smoke.

DALE

A smoke grenade. They thought it would be a good way to announce our arrival.

ALLEN

Right in the middle of meditations . . .

CHEST *(to Allen in audience)*

Hardly an attitude of reverence or respect, would you say?

ALLEN

Neither reverence nor respect was ever pretended as this expedition's forte, Opposer Chest.

PETER

No, not at all.

CHEST

Thank you, Mr. Ginsberg, Mr. Orlovsky . . . let's hope this dampers somewhat the blaze of piety that was about to consume poor Dale; you may resume. Thank you, Miss Tooey.

The lovely denizens of Millbrook mill about the palatial lawn in bikinis. The Spirit smacks his lips:

CASSADY'S SPIRIT

Listen, there's girls everywhere, darling. *Shlurp!* Ho ho oops, pardon me there.

The goosed guard jumps again.

On the KEM Millbrook vanishes and the bus is back in the South.

The golden sun glimpses PORT ARTHOR CITY LIMITS *flashing past. The Pranksters on top of the bus holler for "Liquid! Liquid!" "Piss!" "Gas." "Neal, dammit, pull over!" The bus swings into a gas stop. The crew plays with a band of black kids under the bug-thick service station lights, while the whippoorwills call from the dusk. And the gas pump dings.*

With a roar the pointer moves. Signs flash by in the headlights: SULPHUR *Pop. 2600.* LAKE CHARLES . . . LAFAYETTE. *A Creole fiddle piece reels as the bus rolls. It is Dale, playing wildly on top of the bus. The radio below is competing with snatches of "Shrimp Boats is a-comin' . . ." "Goin' down to Jackson, gonna mess around . . ." "Sun goes down moon comes out; people gather 'round and they all begin to shout: Hey! Hey! Uncle Judd; it's a treat to beat your feet in the—" Zeek. "—and them that plants 'em, are soon forgotten, but Ol' Man Ribber—" Zeek. "—so deep an' wide, long-haired woman on the other side. Now*

she's gone gone but I don't worry. I'm sittin—on top—of the—"
"On my left stood big Joe McKennedy, his eyes were bloodshot
red . . ." The radio continues but the roar, the fluting and
fiddling, have all stopped. Sandy is talking to a fat cop in a
New Orleans patrol car.

SANDY

No, no, nothing to do with integrating anything. Just
going to the World's Fair . . .

The cop is dubious. He looks past Sandy where the radio can
still be heard. "He turned to the crowd behind him, and these
are the very words he said—" A flute joins in on the chorus.
"I went down to the St. James Infirmary. I saw my baby
there . . ." It is Kesey, sitting atop a piling, watching the sun
come up over the Mississippi, fluting along, dolorous and dis-
cordant. . . . "Stretched out on a long white table, so clean, so
cold and so fair. Let 'er go; let 'er go; God bless 'er . . ." A
bunch of black kids watch.

DALE *(voice-over)*

I mean, see, there was no earthly reason for this dip through the deep darky South . . .

The cop pulls away. The crew on the docks watch him leave. ". . . *wherever she may be. She may search this wide world over* . . ."

. . . but it was like part of the tour.

". . . *she'll never find a sweeter man than—*" *Click. Quiet. A boat toots. A piano plays far away.* "*Let's hit the streets,*" *cries Gretch and a colorful crew follows a swaggering Cassady into Sunday morning New Orleans. The church bells ring. The trolley clangs. The plodding, bluesy piano sounds clear. Babbs pauses to jaw with a black picket. Cassady postures before a nut shop with a big sign:* DAD LOVES NUTS.

TOOEY *(voice-over)*

And did you, Dale? find your tour guide into this heart of darkyness?

The piano is louder. It is coming from the door of a bar. The strollers stop.

> **DALE** *(voice-over)*
> Why, I guess we did, praise the Lord. Right in the Heart of New Orleans. In this Canal Street dive . . . the Real Absinthe Bar, I think. He wasn't any darky. He was plenty funky, though.

The group straggles into the bar. Finally, through the gloom, they can make out a white man sitting at the piano. He is wearing suspenders and a porkpie hat. He continues chording with one hand while he takes the cigarette from the corner of his mouth with the other. This hand is stunted and wizened, like an old doll's hand. He puts aside the cigarette and resumes playing with both hands. The Pranksters sit, the window at their backs, the morning sun silhouetting them. The man begins to sing:

> **MOONLIGHT** *(singing)*
> Oh I feel sad and lonely
> Well I feel sad and lonely.
> Oh them people said,
> Them people said,
> "Here comes the big weird bus
> And you've got a long way to go."

> **BABBS** *(applauding from his window seat:)* Big weird bus. Yeah, he's singing it . . .

In the next room the barflies guffaw. Moonlight looks at his audience, solemnly. They are not laughing. They are not looking at his deformed hand. In fact, they are setting up mikes and camera to record his music. He sings to them:

> **MOONLIGHT** *(singing)*
> I wandered round this country.
> I been from town to town.

Seems to me there was always
Some cat that'll put me down,
Someone to put me down.
I love you.
I love you.
Some folks call me trouble.
Some folks call me bad news.
Then there's them real old honest folks
That know I've got the blues.
Oh-h-h-h-h-h-h me.
They know I've got the blues.
I've wandered around this country

Been from town to town—(*becomes self-conscious and stops singing*) and every time I see one of them big tall cameras boy I'm telling you that puts me—I'll—that makes me nervous.

GRETCH

Oh!

MOONLIGHT

A pretty girl.

GRETCH

Wrong.

MOONLIGHT

Where's the nut at?

CASSADY

One block and right down to the corner.

MOONLIGHT

Give me somebody I can look at.

KESEY

Come take a walk over to the bus. Enough sitting around.

MOONLIGHT

Say I want somebody I can look at. I don't want to
look at that thing. You all thinks I'm a nut. Right?

KESEY *(voice-over)*

You were doing a good job before.

MOONLIGHT *(shutting his eyes
and straining to sing again, sweat rolling from his
face:)*

Say bartender,
Say bartender.
Give me *one* time the *same* thing
You gave me one *time* before. . . .
Say bartender,
Give me one time the same time the same thing
You gave me once before.
Because I've had the same damn feeling
Since my baby walked out that door.
I've got the blue-ue-ues
Called midnight.
I've got the blues
From the night, the night before.
I've had the same gone feeling
Ever since my woman walked out the door.

GRETCH

It-it's-it's—

BABBS

Sticky?

GRETCH

Yes, still sticky. I'd say the sticky blues.

MOONLIGHT *(still singing)*

Well I need your love.
I need your love-ov-ove I-I-I nee-ee-eed Your love.

(His music has built to a peak that makes him self-conscious again. Speaking voice:) That stinks. That stinks. *(to Gretch:)* I want you to stand right,—I've got to have somebody to look at: *(singing again:)* Well the Lord made the world—

(talking:) You guys are wasting too much time on me. That stunk.

GRETCH

By whose standards?

MOONLIGHT

By my standards.

GRETCH

The only standards that count. Let's split.

ALL *(voice-over)*

Yeah, split. Split split split.

Moonlight is hustled up from the piano bench and into the furor of departure. The bus door closes behind him and the bus booms off through the New Orleans streets. The gavel bangs. Moonlight, 25 years later, is on the stand, answering the bailiff:

MOONLIGHT

—it isn't my actual name, of course, but what they called me was Moonlight Sinatra.

TOOEY

Whatever for?

MOONLIGHT

Oh, I would venture it was the spiffy little hat. It wasn't my singing, I tell you that for a *fact*. I am no musician. I wasn't even at that piano until the bartender noticed them hanging around outside the place and says, "It's a load of Freedom Riders! I'll pay ten dollars to anybody who'll sing some blues to 'em." —it was a piano bar, you see, and I guess their regular blues man was

eatin' Sunday chicken, or something—and I says, "I'm your boy."

TOOEY

I've heard worse.

MOONLIGHT

I know a couple of chords, but, I'm no musician. Yet, damn me, they sucked it up like sponges; *believed* it; and the more they believed it—you got to appreciate I'd been up four nights and three days. I was running away from my old man; I and my old man ran a welding shop in Biloxi and I'd had a argument with him and told him to shove it, and run off to New Orleans on a weekender bender. I did that on him about once every six months right up till 3 years ago come Mardi Gras, when he had a stroke—the more I believed it.

The bus is racketing along. Gretch wipes at the sweat.

GRETCH

We got to find someplace before I die!

MOONLIGHT

Someplace like what, pretty girl?

GRETCH *(voice-over)*

Someplace like wet.

MOONLIGHT

I will personally guide you . . . to our lovely Lake Pontchartrain . . . let me think . . .

He closes his eyes to think and falls immediately to sleep as the bus bounces on.

MOONLIGHT *(in courtroom)*

Actually, I passed out the instant I hit that bus seat. I didn't wake up until it stopped.

On the bus, Moonlight awakes. He raises his hat and turns to squint out the bus window against which he has been leaning, his rumpled coat for a pillow. He sees an unfocused sign right outside his window.

MOONLIGHT (*voice-over from the courtroom*) But, this stuff you been saying about this driver? he was no slouch! High as he was, he homed that bus in on Pontchartrain just like it was his regular route.

Moonlight-on-the-bus blinks. The sign comes into focus.
PUBLIC BEACH—COLORED ONLY
ORDINANCE 1330
PONTCHARTRAIN COUNTY.

It wasn't precisely the shores I had in mind, but it *was* Pontchartrain.

The crew meanders dreamily across the beach. They are the only white people in sight.

If they *had* been Freedom Riders, doing it with some kind of civil righteousness, some of them black dudes would've took a piece home for dinner, 'stead of chicken! But they wasn't. They was just wasted, and hot, and they just flopped right in, right in the same water as the rest. The big girl, right in her dress. Pregnant as a possum. Everybody could see: these weren't aggravators; these were ignoramusses. That's what saved them.

Ray Charles's "One Mint Julep" blares from the bus-top speakers. It carries over the swimming sounds. The song ends, then passes on to "Hit the Road, Jack." The bus rolls, its footage very red and sped up. Feverish. Even Ray Charles is sped up.

        MOONLIGHT *(voice-over in court)*
I got them to give me a ride to Biloxi. I thought they'd be winding down by dark, but they was just winding up . . .

The interior bus action grows more frenzied, louder. "Freak out, freak out for Jesus," yells Dale.

I was scared at first. But I was broke, and sick—I got the ache from polio—and I needed a ride, so I finally figured: shoot, it's all the same water . . . and, after a while, I went back to sleep.

The fever footage reaches a peak and holds, quiet. We are back in the courtroom.

They liked me. They treated me straight. When we got to Biloxi, they asked me if I wanted to ride along.

        CHEST
Did you?

MOONLIGHT

Want to? Lordy yes: who wouldn't? But there *was* the welding business . . . I was already a day late, and worried about my old man and all, and—

CHEST

That's all. I was just wondering. No more from me; Miss Tooey?

TOOEY

No. Wait. *(Pointing to KEM where a still shows George sitting near the driver's seat:)* Do you know this fellow's name? We haven't talked to him.

MOONLIGHT *(looking,   shaking his head:)* Nope. I don't remember any of the names. I remember that driver, and the big girl, and the big ex-Marine, but I don't even remember seeing this guy, let alone his name.

VOICE *(from audience)*

Hardly Visible.

TOOEY *(looking out)*

What's that?

George, on stand, answering:

GEORGE

George Walker. I got the name Hardly Visible because of my penchant for bright colors.

TOOEY

My name is Miss Tooey, as you probably know. I'd like to ask you—could you tell us a little bit about how you came to be involved with these people, in this particular expedition? Especially Mr. Cassady?

GEORGE

I probably couldn't tell a little bit. I could tell you a lot.

TOOEY

Do your best to be concise.

GEORGE

Well, as briefly as possible . . . it started the previous fall when I was in New York with Mr. Kesey and his brother Chuck, cruising around the site where they were building the set for the World's Fair that was to be in New York in the following summer, 1964. We decided at that time that we would like to come back and see that Fair, bring a few friends. As it turned out that there were so many of us we decided we'd buy a bus. Cassady showed up just 2 or 3 days before the bus was ready to go.

As George recalls Neal his voice begins to gather speed, and the KEM tries to respond, providing rapidly changing impressions of Neal's world—tires; road signs; cars; nighttime speeding and daytime toil; handfuls of white pills—faster and faster . . .

GEORGE *(voice-over)*

He'd been around the scene a lot at night. Days, he was seriously into changing tires up in the city. He had a family to support and everything. Families. But he came past and saw that here's this bunch of crazy kids about to set off across the country and of course if you've read any Kerouac you know that Cassady knew how to travel across the country—: "I gotta take care of you boys you know changing tires, I got this 8-ton jack I got this lug wrench you guys need a lug wrench on this goddamn bus here look I got a couple of spare inner tubes, boot—you never saw a boot

before? goes *inside* the spare on a big tire you know—
we're talking about 10 hundred by twenties on 10-lug
bus you understand it's none of this 5 lugs and whip
off your 15-pound Volkswagen doughnut no thank you
it's about 160 pounds as I recall . . ."

GEORGE *(voice slowing:)*
Anyway, he showed us all this gear and said I gotta
go along and take care of you guys. So that was how
Cassady came along.

TOOEY
Thank you. That was a very thorough brief answer.
What was your initial impression of Mr. Cassady?

GEORGE
I didn't like him.

TOOEY
Why?

GEORGE
I thought he was on a heavy ego trip. I remember he
was standing at a table in a room, in my "pad"—I
was kind of into the cool school, you understand,
everybody sit back and smoke joints, do your cool
thing. Cassady was kicking his seat back and forth
and bouncing up and down and gesturing all over the
place and trying to talk to everybody all at once and
I thought good god who's this guy making all this racket
and trying to overwhelm this whole scene? I thought
he was uncool.

TOOEY
And had your impression of him changed by the time
the bus actually left?

GEORGE
Oh yeah definitely.

TOOEY

In what direction?

GEORGE

Well for one thing I knew he knew how to change tires.

TOOEY

And his driving?

GEORGE *(voice-over)*

It was almost crazy. Look. We're all loaded on acid and trying to throw this ball around as the bus goes careening down the highway at high speed and Cassady seeing how many curbs he can almost hit.

Balls and people bounce off the walls, floor and ceiling of the careening bus, like some kind of sky lab experiment.

TOOEY *(voice-over)*

And how did you all as passengers feel about this behavior on the part of your driver?

GEORGE *(voice-over)*

We all became very close friends, very fast . . .

On KEM the crew dances in a ludicrous conga line, fluting and tooting through the mossy cypress trees.

GEORGE *(hearing fluting on KEM)* This is Babbs's early digs where he was a Marine in Pensacola. We went to this place where his old roommate service buddy still lived.

CHEST

What was the purpose of this dancing?

GEORGE

God only knows. Togetherness . . . maybe art. Look, we're fluting to the ants on the spilled shrimp. This is all very artistic if you look at it in an artistic light. If

Neal was partly our leader it was because he looked at his life in an artistic light. And he was very conscious of the way this outlook affected other people.

CHEST
Isn't that a bit pretentious and egocentric, Mr. Walker?

GEORGE
He wasn't doing it vainly but visionarily. That's why he was so frantic around a lot of people. A lot of people still thought the world was flat.

Back on bus. "Boo-ard!" Bus rolling.

Cassady's already sailed around it, you know what I mean? People'd say, "Watch out man you're gonna fall off." And he'd say,

Inside of bus; crew sitting and riding, dreamily, serenely.

"Hey look man, I've been there 3 times and these are some of the guys I brought back. Indians. They don't look much like Indians but they come from a city of gold with paved streets and built-in sewer systems and thousands of miles of wide straight paved highways."

Shot of Lake. Back in courtroom George interrupts his reverie, watching KEM:

GEORGE *(voice-over)*
Lake Holocaust. Where lightning almost got us. We were having this discussion as to whether lightning would strike a low place like a lakeshore when . . .

BOOM! Lightning crashes into Lake Holocaust scene, changing it to the bus roar at night. Dangerous road out windshield. Sound of not being able to get it into lower gear. Cassady cursing and rapping.

CASSADY *(at wheel)*

Psschoom! Shit. I'm afraid that is a bad rod sound, aye, yes. Well just don't peak out in high there, that's probably the worst part for it.

The bus is picking up speed through the night. The tires squeal and the corners sweep past in the headlights. On top a couple are rousted from their moment of privacy by the glare of a sun gun. They try to shout but the wind is too loud. And the motor roaring. And the tires screeching. They begin climbing to the back turret, worried.

Inside the bus people are being tossed every which way.

In the courtroom the Spirit chortles in demonic glee:

CASSADY'S SPIRIT

The bus twist! You can't help but do it after a couple of curves.

In the driver's seat Cassady is wildy cranking at the wheel. His booted foot is tramping at the useless brake. Behind him the balls are still being bounced about furiously.

GEORGE *(voice-over)*

We felt that it was good to have good reflexes. You never know when something might happen strange right in front of you.

CASSADY *(driving)*

Gotta shift, though. *Ptachoom!* There, that's not so bad. Keep it just under the top. Like important not to miss a shift in a race car. Blow your engine. *Pschoom.*

Over the bus sound, the stereo is beginning to work. Cassady's voice begins to crackle out of the roar.

TOOEY *(voice-over)*

Was the bus something of a cacophony running through the communities of America at that time? did the townspeople object?

GEORGE *(voice-over)*

They didn't object but to call it a cacophony is perhaps the understatement of the decade. Keep in mind that at this time nobody had ever seen a hippie bus or the hippie or the painted anything. People didn't have a pigeonhole to put it into to get uptight about it.

In the aisle of the moving bus a dark-eyed teenager in white bra and panties and beautiful brown skin is being decorated with toothpaste.

.This is Anonymous, the fifteen-year-old Indian girl Hagen kidnapped to take Stark's place. Actually, I'm speaking facetiously. She came quite willingly.

CASSADY'S SPIRIT

I thought she was seventeen or I'd never let her on the bus. Seventeen's all right, officer.

The border guards search the bus. Anonymous stands with the others, watching the search, frowning.

The officials satisfy themselves that the runaway isn't on board and dismiss the bus. It roars off, over a curb. The bunks collapse in a heap. People flounder about the rubble.

GEORGE *(voice-over)*

It often got this way. When we started out this thing was very neat, like a little ship, you know. Cassady's driving was a little heavier than anything you saw on the seven seas. He was just trying to test it out, see, find out where edges were.

CHEST *(voice-over)*

You mean some of the apparent jerkiness one perceives looking at this film is actually deliberate?

GEORGE *(voice-over)*

It rode a little bit smoother than that. Not a lot. They didn't make 'em real smooth back in 1939. Also, Cassady had learned how to drive driving nonsynchromesh crash boxes, Model A Fords. He said he'd probably stolen 500 Model A's by the time he was eighteen.

CHEST *(voice-over)*

Stolen, you say, Mr. Walker?

GEORGE *(voice-over)*

Excuse me. Borrowed. I think he told me one time that he had borrowed 600 cars before he was 16. I feel it must have been some kind of record.

The bus footage is interspersed with snapshots of young Neal driving, leaning against cars, looking at cars . . .

CHEST *(voice-over)*

And was Mr. Cassady proud of having borrowed 600 cars?

GEORGE *(voice-over)*

How else was he going to learn how to drive? He was born poor. His father was a skid row alcoholic bum in the Depression in Denver.

From snapshots of cars driving, to color shots of cars driving, back to bus driving.

If you like to drive then you can sympathize. I like to drive. I stole cars and I was born wealthy. I love to drive more than most. Cassady loved to drive more than *anybody*. You have to understand what it was

he was trying to accomplish. It was more than just getting there. It had to do with the *trip*, which had to do with the movie, and the effect that he was trying to create . . . on people's minds. Of doing something that was out on the edge. It *was* exciting. The bus was attempting to be a moving carnival of sorts. So a man who could drive it like a carny ride was obviously your most valued driver, right?

CHEST *(voice-over)*

Well, I'd have to leave it to you to tell me what driving was important.

GEORGE *(voice-over)*

Exciting driving. Otherwise we'd have taken the Greyhound.

A car honks and passes. Cassady raps "—beer belly Nellie, you knew her by her belly . . ." The little radio plays. The bus grinds hard up a hill. A sign flashes in the headlights for an instant: SMOKEY MOUNTAINS—SUMMIT—STEEP GRADE. TRUCKS AND BUSSES USE LOWER GEAR. "Registered as a house car, sir; not a bus . . . ," Cassady mutters, then down the grade he heads, still stomping at the worthless brake.

GEORGE *(voice-over)*

Over the Smokies. Down the Blue Ridge Parkway with all the brakes burned out. Oh man, what a ride. Cassady wired like a time bomb: "Gotta make New York before it closes down Friday. Brakes gone, no matter. We can coast there in a day and a half." He was knighted after that ride; Sir Speed Limit. I think that was the first run that scared everybody. I remember times when it was clear off the road and people jumpin' down the hatch with their eyes lookin' like saucers: "This is the end!" Sometimes I think he planned it that way. He'd done that road once before and knew the escape route.

   CASSADY (*driving through the terrified night:*) Here's Go! Go! Go! Go! Go! And they'll set a new track course overcoming everybody. How's that for a finish? There you have it, a typical Hollywood nowhere idea. I mean I did it that way because how else can I think? Ha ha. No no no that's not the idea at all. We'll go into *that* system later, ho ho ho. We're making movies right now. Movies, that's what counts!

The careening bus finally misses the turn. Tires squeal and people scream. The words ESCAPE ROUTE *flash in the headlights. The bus goes bumping safely up the escape ramp.*

Back in the courtroom, Tooey is shaking her head.

TOOEY
Did it make people angry at him?

GEORGE
Kesey used to break out and say "All right, that's it!" And he was gonna point to somebody and say "You drive now!" But he'd look around, and look around again, and there was nobody else that was even *close* to ready to drive.

In full daylight, the bus is pulling out of a turnpike toll plaza. The Howard Johnson's roof gleams against the sky. A truck roars past.

CASSADY
Bo-ard! And I also want J.B. to know, any ordinary man would've at least taken a piss or washed the bugs out've his eyes after a cup of coffee, but not me.

GEORGE *(watching the KEM dreamily, smiling at the grind of gears:)* I just wish he'd learned to shift.

CASSADY

Goddammit!

Cassady finally hits low gear and the bus eases out onto the road.

CASSADY

Atlantic City Electric Company says it's twenty to eleven, Jane. George Washington Bridge. Guess that's highway 40, no? No, that's the tunnel. I'll go on 40 to Atlantic City anyhow, huh?

GEORGE *(voice-over)*

Damn. America! Driving right on through. Neal-at-the-wheel America . . .

CASSADY

Welcome to New Jersey, speed fifty. New Jersey Turnpike. *(sings)* I don't worry 'cause we're on the turnpike now.

George's voice in courtroom begins to fade into bus roar. He shouts against the roar but continues growing fainter until he is just a background voice on bus.

GEORGE *(voice-over)*

You're up here driving the bus in front of everybody and you gotta keep talking about something. All the time. Keep it going. Keep it interesting. Straight road, you move it back and forth a little, anything you can do, just keep it happening . . .

CASSADY

C'mon car. That's better. Woman. Perfectly sound. Still got her left blinker on.

GEORGE *(on bus)*

Gonna turn sometime.

CASSADY

Yeah. Ha ha, what a brain. George, if you do that one more time, you'll have to be a disciple. *(He shifts and clunks the gear.)* Goddammit. New York, one hundred! That old woman had her dress above her knee hee hee—New York, one hundred! I think it was her knee. She's pretty old. *Cshhh!* Felt that one, ha ha ha. Hi baby. Hey-ell, I'm going to get friendly today. *Cough.* Ease off. *Csshhh.* . . . New York! Somewhere north. Dig this semi passing. This forces me behind the other semi. Oh but the lane widens permanently it seems to three lanes, sir, aye that it does. Well I'll have to shift down for him sirrah, no no no, all right *kaboom.* He had buck teeth, too! It seems to grow in the South. You remember Carol Baker? Yes, oh yes, well, easy on, there. Ease off on that rev here. Stop that! Go back to fourth! All right, sir, *shoom!* Jaazus . . .

Now Oldsmobile nemesis. It always seems to be, I don't know why. Oldsmobile. First car I stole, perhaps that's it, ha ha ha.

(Trying to light a joint) Come on now, you're not even interested yet . . . *(coughs)* it is—it slipped off the guard. We'll leave it there right at the moment, 'cause I'm in 4th—nice work, working nicely. The teacher that taught me to say it had buck teeth like that southern truck driver! New York Seventy! New Yaw-w-wk! We've always had the wind from the left, isn't that weird?

All right, I'll bring it down. Bring it down gently. Gotta bring it down. *(sniffs)* I think the elementals are getting through! They get through in a continuing pattern. In other words: in every force, in every world, in every

stream, in every *structure*—like, say a road—its weakest link, the road is no better than its weakest link, you see? In every action or thing like *pshhoooo!* there's a weak spot. Now that weak spot is always attacked by the highest of the next lower forces. Like second dimensional, third dimensional, fourth dimensional. . . . worlds separate, but worlds that still touch—second, third that touches second and fourth, fourth that touches fifth and—See there's three dimensions of space & three dimensions of time—fourth, fifth and six is time, then, the fourth dimensional concept of time. It, what actually *is* is our subconscious or soul, mind, or thought, our consciousness even is in that same fourth dimension . . .

Over his voice, and through the roar of the turnpike, a siren becomes audible, coming nearer.

We are actually *fourth* dimensional beings in a *third* dimensional body inhabiting a *second* dimensional world!

A red light flashes in the rearview.

Pull over? *Balagghhh!* Now, as far as the smoking and everything—

GEORGE

We've been stopped! We've been stopped!

Panic. Zonk spills the rolling box. George waves at the smoke. The Day-Glo orange juice is slammed back in the refrigerator. Scrambling around on the floor Zonk remembers the joint behind his ear and eats it. The bus stopped, Neal stands to confront the situation.

CASSADY

We have the smoking—? Good. No no no, I'm perfectly all right. . . . Who's gotten on the top and the back?

JANE

Nobody was on the top.

ZONK

We were on the back, though.

CASSADY

Back in the bus! Back in the bus!

Hagen has already made it off the bus with the camera. He films first the patrol car, then Kesey coming out the bus door with a portable tape recorder spewing tape, then a tall, imposing New Jersey Highway Patrolman. With a stern thumb the cop sends Kesey jumping back on the bus, then turns on Hagen. He speaks directly into the camera. No words can be heard but his intent is obvious, and the filming stops abruptly.

GEORGE *(in courtroom)*

We all thought, "Fuck. Inches from our goal and busted!" All that guy had to do was stick his New Jersey nose inside and our little trip was terminated.

Inside the bus the crew exchange worried looks. The freeway traffic snarls past. Cassady can be seen in the patrol car ahead, gesturing in an earnest frenzy.

GEORGE *(voice-over)*

But, once again . . .

The bus is rolling, pulling cautiously back out onto the turnpike. Cassady eyes the rearview: the cop is following.

CASSADY *(voice-over)*

We talked even intimate. And we shook hands, you notice? Get that on film? No?

Now there's one thing—and this is serious. Not a leg. Not a *foot*! The fuckin' law in this state; you can't even sleep in the backseat with your feet out the window. Hunh-*nnnhh!* Boh-*hard*. You got to stay *inside* from here on! In the South you fear for your life. Here *they* fear for your life! Riding through Texas—hanging out—squirming—your head around bridges I pass—close but not too close—that's why I didn't tear your head off—!

The bus is picking up speed. The cop in the rearview is dropping back. Cassady is feeling better:

CASSADY *(singing)*

You are my sunshine, my only—*(talking)* Concerto: New Jersey Turnpike. Written, composed, and instantaneously conducted and performed backwards. *(tries to toot the flute handed him)* The fucking thing is backwards! Ladies and gentlemen this Kesey bus is so messed up that the flute's backwards! There. Now. Is there a toke commander?

As the commander lights up . . . Tootle tootle! That's the french horn. Tootle tootle ootle. You know that one. Tootle tootle. That was variations on that one.

No one was there, but I waved anyhow. Just in case. He was fucking her with only his eyes above the dashboard. Tootle ootle ooo.

Speeders lose licenses. Too-too-too-toot. Concerto *de la passing diesel*. Wee weee weee weee weee. And a hot red galaxy. Wheet. One moment—*(tweet)*. There's another diesel! Oh, he's behind me. I wondered why he didn't pass. Well! I have someone to stay ahead of. Here he comes. Tooweeeo.

GEORGE

What'd you tell the cop?

CASSADY

Ohhhh. Well, I suppose for once I'll have to answer. Course, I realized the best thing in *all* these short time bits, especially under my present mood, is running commentary. So while he's fiddling and thinking, covering by writing and so on, you're changing his judgment at *one-thirtieth of a second!* In that changing of judgment there's no imposition. He's still the boss. Now stop all that abstraction, Cassady! What'd you say? Well all right. We've come clear across country and within *miles* of the goal, *here*, the first ticket. In fact, after all that trouble in the South—"And I walked through lanes of *cow*boys, sir; we were refused service! Like, even in Phoenix, the reason we got 'A vote for Barry is a vote for fun' is because these boys, yasss . . . hanging out? well, first time in New York every one of them!" . . . and *that's* why they got away with it! I'm sure because *(voice changing)* "Ahem, after the difficulties of the South it's rather strange and I think a fact to be *prized* that the solitary ticket and the *only trouble* we had was home in New Jersey! I'm conductor on a railroad, broke my leg, yeah . . . in fact, as a railroad man and safety factor, I myself

from personal fear have *never* put my foot, as you described officer, out the rear window sleeping *pshoom* and I understand the severities there, the degrees—."

He said, "What do you mean, what do you mean? You guys political? What do you mean? Are you a mixed crowd?" "No no no. Not even political."

Boy his eyes came right with me, all the way. And he was talking with me like a *brother*! Nothing personal, nothing suspicious. He was officious all to the end, but his eyes softened and he was, uh—"Now this is just a warning. There's only one thing: don't let it happen again—that's what the warning's for, see." As soon as I said "No ticket—" he had started to write my name. I saw him pause again. I was in the portion—let me recall a little better, chronologically—of his third movement, major portion, critical point of decision. He starts to write my name, making—and I felt . . . I'll tell you why it went over: because up my spine came the kundalini again, not the kundalini as a pur-ified, the *real* kundalini, the transcendent, of course not! See, we are living, gentlemen, by the four lower centers of the endocrine glands; the centers of force; the ductless glands; the sex glands; the gonads; and the adrenals, and, uh, thymus, thyroid, yes. Then the pineal, pituitary and the head. Well the pineal is fos-silized, that's why *we're not plants*. Well anyhoo . . . what happens is, it goes up on those centers, up the spine, and I felt it. The same feeling you have you know when a chill goes up your spine? And I had the intensity, I had the emotion, I had the power, and I knew I had him! Right there!

I saw he had N-E-A in my first name, and I said, "Now wait a minute!" Oh, the tone! The resignation! The tone as the fire went up me. Loss! That's what it was. It was the reaction of *loss* that gave this chill up the

spine, that's it! I got indignant! As he still had not
written A in the word Neal, I said, "Here I am! I
mean, I'm no virgin! I'm forty years old driving a
thirty-nine—been driving for years! It's not that I
haven't been stopped *before* for driving! And, here's
the ironies. The matching ludicrousy! The first ticket.
The only trouble we had on the trip, as they'll all ask
us, from debutante to showgirl, is—" I didn't say debutante to showgirl, but every other word is verbatim,
"—is not only *being stopped*, our only trouble came
in New Jersey, but that I! innocent victim of these
young boys' desires and first time in New York! if I
haven't yet imparted this to you, sir—" I didn't say
sir though. "—they're a bit out of their minds!" *Noo*
York, Seventy, *Noo* York! Tweeeeeee! Pass. All right.
Here we go. One-handed delight. No no no. That's
masturbating. No no no. That's a Lincoln. That's good
enough. You put fifteen-inch wheels on . . . tootle
wheet. . . . All right for you, diesel, for you only sir
pa-*choom* too-tootle-tootle-tootle. Back again? *Pa-
chow! (glimpses a cigarette billboard)* Kent. Pfoo-
toot. Smoke Kent. Do you know the real name of the
Shadow? No one knows.

VOICE *(from bus crew)*

Lamont—

CASSADY

It's *not* Lamont Cranston, sir. That's one of his many
aliases. It is Kent. K-E-N-T, first name, Kent. Second
name, Allard, like the airplane engine. A-double ell-
A-R-D. Kent Allard, a wealthy playboy skine, skun,
S-C-I-O-N, son of a prominent social—

JANE

Scion.

CASSADY

—scion of a prominent family—wealthy—who went to Peru and under the training of his Indian mystic Tibetan transplant . . . this Tibetan-like Peruvian Indian loaded on coca leaves, no doubt, ha ha ha. And tweetle-tweet-tooweet why did the Cobra outgun the Shadow at the end of part two? Because ha ha ha ha the Shadow toot-tootle-tweet was in the *Cobra uniform* ha ha ha hahaha! Tweetle-tweetle tweet. Another first ha ha. Tweetle tweetle tweet. On the other hand Doc Savage had done it many times with the Monk and the others. And as far as an authoritarian figure need, I even had the Spider, ha ha. Toweeeee. When I was ten, too. Mother dead you know. I decided I had to take care of Father. So, sure enough, I was thirteen; his old lady at the time had a couple of boys older than me, but first orgasms and all you know, thirteen and a half . . . and uh so I ran away from home after she accused me of losing the meat books. Not the meat but the stamps, WPA stamps, food, tweet. Two dollars and thirty cents it was. Just the excuse I needed. Tweet. So it happens that when Massachusetts began as one of the thirteen colonies, ah John Fitzgerald, that we first saw the possibility of your demise, the white brotherhood. Ah yes. You see with black magic rites, you got to have the voodoos and you got to have the witches tale (tail) and the cockroach juice and all that . . . in California it's accepted to drive in the middle lane at the conventional truck speed, yessir it's a point of contention, a point of law, 1953, Adams versus State. Sunday the 28th? well, that would be— we might have to leave Sunday morning then—that's bad. Delay leaving till Sunday night that'd be just right. 24 hours later leaving Kalamazoo, I mean St. Louis Blues and so on. East Saint Louis toodle ooo,

boop boop a doo, waa waa waa waa tweet tweet tweet
tweet Go go go Navy tweet tweet tweet and Penn State
tweet Carolina Al-U-Minium Union North Carolina,
we went through Union tweetle tweetle tweet. Zick.
Strict. Strick, like in the strict discipline, and there
is strict like I was thinking of it: sick strict stricken
tweet tweet strick but mainly more like *Arsenic and
Old Lace*. Strychnine, nine tweet, like a cat. Exit nine.
Next exit, nine miles. Get that on film; forget it. Exit
9, next exit 9, although it says 2 miles, but that's the
standard tweet. The Romans, of course, had the fur-
long *(laughs)* tweet as many like, horses still retain.
28 miles 220 yards or tweet—Thank you officer—calling attention to himself unnecessarily Cassady pro-
ceeded north. Exit nine. Love Potion number nine. I
thought they left off about that love potion. *Cough
cough.* I lost love potion number nine. But anyhow,
the voodoo then, the black magic is . . . when I first

said number nine I knew that that's what I'd refer back to again. But really I was planning myself on the viewing of the exit nine sign which led to love potion and so on . . . But the association, I purposely rejected after that clause and gave another clause so that everyone would be more with me when I mentioned the number nine again and then went back to the voodoo and . . . New Jersey Turnpike Authority. Exit Nine. We finally made it. Now we can get off that rut and go on to another level. New York.

Neal takes a long pull from the joint handed him. Removes it and searches for the orange juice, the joint sticking from between the fingers of his leather glove.

"There's only one thing," he sez. "Don't let it happen again!" That's what the warning's for, see? He had the finish and he had the out too, y'see. And he did his duty. There's nobody on the roof or outside, is there? No. *Psshooo!* and there's no breaking of the law.

Neal soothes his throat with a swig of orange juice.

TOOEY

So would you say, George, that Mr. Cassady looked out for you?

GEORGE

Like we were his own kids. He *knew* New York, see— *(responding to footage on KEM:)* Look, Harlem! we were a big hit in Harlem—from his Kerouac-and-Ginsberg days, and we were his family he was gonna show what the city was all about. The—ta-da—*Big Apple!*

GEORGE *(voice-over)*
Hey look! There's Neal busting us into that apartment on 73rd—

CHLOE *(to Jane seated beside her in the courtroom:)* Right-o. Like a pig to a pantry.

GEORGE *(voice-over)*
—where we rendezvoused with Kerouac and the East Coast element. That's Peter Orlovsky's crazy brother, Julius. His first trip out of the nut house in twelve years and this is the world he finds. A historic bash. Freaks meet beats! East meets West! High meets—

CHEST
Before we become further intoxicated by these exotic distances, Mr. Walker, didn't you say Mr. Cassady had a family back home? How was he looking out for them?

As George answers, Chest's assistant approaches with a note and hands it to the opposer.

GEORGE

Yeah, he used to ask for money—to send home . . . to his wife and kids.

CHEST

And your hero could look you in the eye and do *that*?

Chest unfolds the note, smiling as he reads it.

GEORGE

He was demeaned by it, but sure; Cassady could look you in the eye and do anything, be completely embarrassed about it then in an instant be flying high, wide and wailing again. In the breakneck instant. But I'll tell you; being the hero, he had to always try to *outdo* the hero. And that can take its toll, even on superheroes. So, every now and then he'd have to retreat someplace and clean up—someplace like Mexico—get the speed out of his system so he could do it all again.

TOOEY

Excuse me, George. I'd like to interrupt a moment to speak with Mr. John Page Browning. No, Mr. Browning, you don't have to come up. You are still under the auspices of this inquiry.

Page is sitting up very straight in his dark shroud. He looks toward the KEM, where the crew is gathered outside a bullring.

TOOEY *(voice-over)*

You mentioned you were in Mexico, where Mr. Cassady—

PAGE *(voice-over)*

That's me! Outside the Tijuana bullring waiting for my contact! The mother jumper. And Neal. But he

wasn't—I mean this wasn't the place in Mexico where Cassady died. Or the time. This is Tijuana! Where I became Des Prado because this pimp dealer he—

> TOOEY *(voice-over)*
> Mr. Browning, in the interest of expediency, where and when in Mexico did Mr. Cassady die?

The bullfighter approaches the exhausted bull, pulling the bright sword from its cape. The bull lowers its head for a last charge.

> PAGE *(voice-over)*
> In San Miguel de Allende. Some time later. Where he'd gone to woodshed.

> TOOEY *(voice-over)*
> Woodshed?

> PAGE *(voice-over)*
> Like George said, to clean up.

TOOEY *(voice-over)*

Apparently he didn't get into the right laundry this time.

Cassady's Spirit has leaned close to the guard, narrating the bullfight action for her as she watches the KEM, rapt.

CASSADY'S SPIRIT

Dig that horn. *Watch this.* Look at this guy bleed. I know all about bullfighting, darling.

A gloved hand appears on her inner thigh, moving up. She continues to watch the bullfight, breathing through parted lips.

Why that bull hasn't even lowered his head yet! Got to get his head down. Aurgh! The banderillas. Cutting those muscles. I'll not yet deign to make my entrance.

The gloved hand has found her belt buckle.

The bull paws the sand.

PAGE *(voice-over)*

What I hear around Limbo, somebody dared him to count the railroad ties on the track between San Miguel and the next town. So he headed out—with a pack of Camels, a bottle of tequila and no shirt. The next town thirty miles away and Cassady was going to count the ties . . .

CASSADY'S SPIRIT

It's a very nice kill as I remember. Ooargh! Lovely lovely. The poor fellow. Wouldn't quit showbiz.

The bull drops, coughing blood. In the bleachers, the bus crew applauds. In the courtroom they watch the KEM soberly.

A railroad crew found him in the morning and took him to the hospital back in San Miguel. Where he died, they tell me. Of hypothermia, they tell me.

The bull is dragged away by the horses, leaving a smooth road through the sand with a red line down the center.

TOOEY
Were there any last words?

PAGE
They tell me there was. But like I say, I wasn't there.

TOOEY
Thank you, Mr. Browning. I trust I can excuse you . . . for the purposes of *this* inquiry, anyway. Mr. Chest? Any further questions?

CHEST *(pocketing note)*
For Mr. John Page Browning? Not at present. But with the court's permission, the opposition would like to reopen its case to call one last witness.

Tooey turns just in time to see door of courtroom closing after admitting this final witness. She squints, straining to see who it is.

CHEST *(voice-over)*
Miss Stark Naked to the stand please.

Stark is a striking woman with shining black hair and eyes, and a mature bearing that makes many of the previous witnesses seem by comparison more than a little silly.

The spirit has all but dragged the guard into the dock. He pauses for a look at the surprise witness.

CASSADY'S SPIRIT
Stark Naked in tights! Yasss, seven o'clock delights . . .

The bailiff is interested. His eyes widen as she approaches. He straightens his wig and rises grandly to administer to her.

BAILIFF
How would you be called?

STARK

I would be called Katrina Daniels. And you?

The bailiff stands, open-mouthed. Chest intervenes with a confident sweep of his hand.

CHEST

If you would be seated, Katrina. Make yourself comfortable. Perhaps you recognize some of these people in our court. Old friends?

STARK

I recognize some of them, yes. It's been a long time.

CHEST

How long?

STARK

Twenty-five years.

CHEST

A stretch, even by this court's standards. But surely your roads have crossed since that initial run, with some of your old busmates?

STARK

No intersection for decades.

CHEST

My my. Well, be that as it may, let's get on to the incident in question. Might I say, you seem quite sensible, Katrina. How did you let yourself become involved in this voyage? Were you shanghaied?

STARK

I was hypnotized.

CHEST

Go on.

STARK

The whole entourage appeared at my house one day and danced around my apartment. There was just a great deal of general joviality and laughing and dancing. Like a troupe of minstrels.

CHEST

So how did they present the idea of a bus trip to you? What were you expected to do? Or offered.

STARK

Well, Ken Kesey said that he was interested in making a movie of a group of people and their personalities and the interaction between them, *laissez-faire*. It suited my mood exactly at the moment—

CHEST

When did you first see Mr. Cassady?

STARK *(going on)*

—yet somehow I began to feel alienated. They were all artists, and authors and professors. And this made me feel even more—I mean if there was any group of people in the world that would be mine, where I felt I should belong and fit in . . . but I didn't. And I was starting to leave. I walked away from the house and there was this little piddling creek with this little bridge and I was standing feeling sad and uncertain and all of a sudden out pops this man almost from nowhere, for all the world like an Irish leprechaun. Then he opened his mouth and said about forty words and immediately everything was all funny and meaningful. Of course I knew nothing of Neal Cassady then. I believe I'd read *On the Road* but even if I'd heard the name I wouldn't have related to it. It was the sheer impact of this man's love of living that captivated me.

CHEST

Hypnotized—

TOOEY

Hang on, Chest. Katrina, what was there about this man that produced this strong feeling? Was it something ominous?

STARK

Not at all. He was so sparkly. His eyes twinkled with mischief.

CHEST

When you boarded the bus did the sense of alienation you had at the party return perhaps in increase?

STARK

It would vary greatly. I always felt the closest to Neal.

CHEST

Why?

STARK

I think it was just my tremendous trust of him.

CHEST

Is that why you drank a double dose of the drug he gave you?

STARK

I didn't—I don't remember.

CHEST

Well, let's see if this can refresh your memory.

The bus is in the sand again, Stark standing in the door with her flute. At Wikieup.

STARK

Oh, I thought—oh god . . . were we loaded. Oh I remember going into town and getting food and stuff, yeah.

CHEST

The film indicates that you brought back a lobster tail and saltines.

STARK

Right. I think I mentioned I was tired of ratburgers and they probably were getting on my case and saying all right you go and buy the food then. I remember later on, in the the desert I think, taking the other food I'd bought, the melons and the tomatoes, and putting them in the sand to better realize their tremendous beauty. Like a baby. That was me playing the mandolin all through there, huh? Not too bad.

CHEST

Do you remember this crying?

STARK

Those guys *were* really giving me a hard time. I thought I was imagining things. No wonder I went gah gah.

CHEST

Let's listen again to some of the exchanges you two were having.

The center screen of the KEM runs the conversation as left and right offer subtitles:

NEAL	STARK
	Did you ever kill someone?
No, I didn't, but I thought that the threat of course, worse than the execution, would be just enough to destroy that illusion . . . but I see you're held in violence. Better than rocks, and cuts, and glass.	The sun's coming up and we're—it's a gun, that's what it is. *(singing)* And how longgg can it go on, how longgg can we wait for help, when no help is

coming forth, and Jean-Paul Sartre is dead, oh yes . . . oh, yes; yes, that's all you must do.

Oh, if it gets that far, you really need help.

Oh, what a savior. Oh, help me, oh fart.

CHEST

Weren't you getting paranoid here?

STARK *(watching)*

I *am* making a lot of allusions to death.

CHEST

Isn't it obvious that he's trying to press you back onto the subject of a possible sexual rendezvous here, whether or not it is to your liking or even your well-being?

STARK

Oh, probably.

CHEST

You said you had a headache. He said "I'll get you a few aspirins I've been saving just for you. The last girl took 50. It wasn't quite enough. I thought a hundred." Are you aware of the number of women who committed suicide over this man?

STARK

Four. I don't think I took any of this stuff very seriously.

CHEST

Do you think upon reflection that perhaps he was interested in manipulating you, seducing you, getting you within his mental or telepathic powers?

STARK

He already *had* me in his telepathic powers. It was nice . . . like being in an invisible fun house.

CHEST

We've had testimony here indicating that during your sojourn in that fun house you became actually more and more miserable. As well as visible.

STARK

It was very hot in the bus. Actually, I started wearing this blanket.

CHEST

Because it was so hot?

STARK

No, because my suitcase came open on top and a lot of my clothes blew away.

CHEST

Do you recall how the window of this bus got broken?

STARK

No, why?

CHEST

You don't recall running out into the thorns, topless? Tell us what you *do* recall in Houston, then, that led to your abandonment.

STARK

I wasn't abandoned. I was arrested.

CHEST

Because of the spectacle of your arrival?

STARK

Oh, you're talking about *that* incident. Where Larry came out to the bus. He was carrying his child and it reminded me of my daughter. I guess I tried to hold the child.

CHEST

Were you wearing anything?

STARK

I think I dropped the blanket in my excitement.

CHEST

Weren't you worried about alarming the father?

STARK

I'm sure he'd been alarmed before.

CHEST

You were naked on a suburban street in Houston!

STARK

I was back in my blanket before anybody noticed . . .

Stark is wandering away down a leafy street, her bare feet showing from beneath the blanket.

STARK *(voice-over)*

. . . but that wasn't it anyway. I saw this police car pull up and they say Hey sister, come over here. Like two thugs. I straightened my spine and kept walking. The next thing I knew they had thrown me to the ground and handcuffed me. They kept asking me my name and address and slapping me around because I wouldn't answer. But the only address I knew in Houston was Larry's. And I didn't want to give the police that address—not the way those people were acting, with all that pot and stuff on the bus . . . not in Texas twenty-five years ago—so I decided not to say anything. They eventually decided I was a Mexican—I was very tan—maybe an illegal alien who couldn't speak English, maybe even a crazy illegal alien . . .

TOOEY

And because you wouldn't give out the location of your friends the police put you in a hospital?

STARK

In a cell with a woman in restraints. She never stopped screaming or crying. I was there three days and she never stopped and nobody ever came to see her. I don't know how on earth I got a message out to Larry's house. By the time he got out himself—apparently he was pretty distraught-looking when he found me—and got a lawyer to get me out, they were long gone.

CHEST

Were you relieved—?

STARK

I suppose. And a little hurt . . .

CHEST

—relieved to find the pressure of this man's infernal psychic powers at last abated, were you not?

STARK

A little. It can be very disconcerting to have someone around who can read your mind . . . even influence it.

CHEST

Had already influenced it?

STARK

Yes.

CHEST

Twisted it, perhaps crippled it, perhaps, for—

TOOEY

Katrina, Chest is trying to force you to admit to force. Listen to me: did Mr. Cassady ever attempt to oblige

you, by any means whatsoever, physically or psychi-
cally, to do anything that was against your own will?

STARK

You mean to get me in the sack.

TOOEY

So to speak, yes.

STARK

Not as much as I wish he'd tried.

TOOEY

Why?

STARK

Because it would have been very interesting.

RICHY *(from audience)*

Don't you see she's still afflicted? What else can she
say? The tortured is compelled to believe in the good-
ness of the torturer.

DOCTOR KNOT

Ah-h, banana oil.

STARK

I didn't say he was good. But who can anybody here
think of that was more interesting? From that time,
who? Bobby Dylan? Abbie Hoffman? *(she begins to
laugh)* Timmy Leary Johnny Lennon Normy Mailer
Jerry Ruby?

*She breaks off in a long reel of derisive laughter. The sound
rings against the courtroom walls, shrill and reminiscent of her
crazed laughing at Wikieup. Everyone waits uncomfortably until the fit subsides. The atmosphere is left strained by Stark's
outburst. Is she hopelessly twisted after all? Chest approaches
her and asks in genuine concern:*

CHEST

Don't you think you would have done better with a more stabilizing influence during this period in your development, Miss Daniels?

STARK

Neal believed in letting people try their wings, it is true. There were bound to be some crashes . . .

CHEST

Thank you, Miss Daniels.

TOOEY

And the rest of you for your patience.

After Stark returns to her seat.

BAILIFF

That's it then?

TOOEY

The defense has no more questions.

CHEST

God forbid any more from the opposition.

BAILIFF

A verdict, then?

Bangs gavel. But the V-meter barely quivers.

WHITE GLOVE

Give us a mo', Chief. I think she's going to need a shot, first.

The V-meter technician looks back toward dim maintenance area.

CHEST *(picking up the still-smoking ashtray and cigar, moving it near:)* This is more a squeaker than I anticipated. Care to put a bottle on the verdict?

Tooey's assistant comes up with another rose-colored note. Chest starts to look but is startled by a glang.

A glang? Yes, and a loud one. It is the hood of the bus being thrown open. Two rubber-gloved hands bring two huge electrodes against each side of motor block. Sparks fountain from the hood. In the background these sparks are echoed by lightning flashes from tesla coils and Jacob's ladders left over from Bride of Frankenstein.

> **WHITE GLOVE** *(examining dial:)*
> Twist 'er tail!

> **RUBBER GLOVE** *(thumbing   down button on celenoid:)* Twisting here, Chief.

The motor pops. The needle jumps. The lightning flashes.

Tooey, trying to ignore the clamor, reads her note by the light of those flashes.

> **CHEST**
> Ah, the famous last-minute last words? Too late, I fear.

The bus has started, but the ancient motor is smoking and backfiring a tremendous hubbub. The spirit jumps with every bang. So do the V-meter dials.

> But I'm curious, nonetheless . . . what were they?

Tooey looks up from her note.

> **TOOEY**
> Pardon me?

> **CHEST**
> His *expression finale* . . . was there any?

The spirit, taking advantage of the distractions, climbs from the defendant's dock.

CASSADY'S SPIRIT

    Here, boys, let me smooth the old bitch out for you.

He moves toward bus door. No one notices. The attendants are busy with their machine. The guards are fascinated by the fireworks. Chest is retrieving his ashtray preparatory to enjoying the last inch of his cigar after the inquiry is decided.

Tooey has looked back down at her note.

TOOEY

    Yes. In the emergency room. In San Miguel. Two of the gang he was staying with and an old Mexican janitor were present.

Cassady's Spirit has reached the controls. His right hand shakes itself free of the sleeve. It is gloved.

CASSADY'S SPIRIT

    Little too rich first thing after a long nap, huh honey? Just ease it to ya . . .

The gloved hand unlimbers like a concert pianist's, then adjusts the choke. His booted foot comes from beneath the hem of the robe and tromps down on the gas. The stuttering of the engine is replaced by a terrific roar. Rubber Glove jumps upright, bumping his head on the hood. It slams with a bang. He barely gets his rubber gloves back out of the way. Rubbing his head he glares up toward the driver's window, preparing to chew somebody's ass, but is stopped mouth-wide at the demonic sight of Cassady's face glittering over the dash.

Back in the bus cab, the spirit's hand leaves the choke and reaches for the gear. His other foot tromps the clutch.

CASSADY'S SPIRIT

    . . . see how you cotton to a leetle gear ka-chshOOM!

The shift knob is slapped forward. The gears clash with a galvanizing ring. It vibrates the whole courtroom.

Tooey and Chest turn, startled. The bus shimmers a moment, glowing hotter, the vibration getting higher and higher. The flat tire is filling, sucking in air, bringing the bus back upright, then pha-TWANGGG! . . . it explodes into a smoking, sparking, gleaming, completely restored Superbus.

Among the witnesses there is a moment of wonder, but only a moment. Everyone recognizes immediately that the only escape for that bus is straight down the aisle toward the door in back. Like the Red Sea the throng begins to part as the bus comes on. In slow motion it plows through the courtroom toward the door which is much too small; people scramble and pews splinter before the gleaming bumper. The whole wall cracks when it hits the door; the bright light of outside can be seen through the cracks.

The wooden door and white blocks spread to absolute, dimensionless white light . . . then the bus grill, then the cab, then the whole bus, going by very close, and rising, revealing the complete underside, rising and banking, almost past, still slow, then: ptu-ton! back to regular speed, rocketing off, banking up, up and away into traditional Star Wars stretched-out super-movie hyper-space.

Spectators rise from the debris. They stare after the bus through the ragged arch left by the escape. From its two cables, still attached under the hood, the V-meter dangles, spinning.

RUBBER GLOVE
He's got my apparatus!

The cables part and the V-meter falls, just a speck, somersaulting through an ambiguous space, cables flailing . . .

CHEST   *(watching open-mouthed, holding the ashtray:)* Unprecedented.

TOOEY

Sixty-four thousand nine hundred and twenty-eight.

CHEST

Hah?

TOOEY *(smiling, reading from her rose-colored note:)* Sixty-four thousand nine hundred and twenty-eight.

She grins at him, then puts the cigar stub in her mouth for a long, triumphant drag.

CHEST *(looking after the diminishing bus:)* Unprecedented.

Inside the bus, Cassady with hood back, is talking. He turns to grin and the bus spins on, his image winking in the clouds.